FWOOOSH
FWOOO~
SCREECH!
CLAK
CRNCH
CRNCH
I0742085
DOCTOR BALTHIS, M.D
It Had to be You
by Captain Nikko

KOFF
KOFF
MM... HRM..?
GASP!
BLINK!
WHAT THE-
HOW THE FUCK DID I- NO, WHERE THE FUCK AM I?!
...HOLY SHIT.
KRKL
KRK
DUMMMMM DA-TEE-DUMMM...
TINK!
CLINK!
SOMEONE ELSE IS HERE...IS THAT A KITCHEN?
IS THERE A DRAFT IN HERE..?
FLOP!
!
WHERE THE FUCK ARE MY CLOTHES?!

ALRIGHT, THAT DOES IT.
I GOTTA FIND OUT WHO TOOK MY SHIT!
IF THEY TRY ANYTHING I'LL GRAB A KNIFE...
WAIT-
SOMETHING SMELLS...GOOD?
SNIFF SNIFF.
SSSSSSSSSSSSSSS.....
HUMMMM-DA DEE-DUMMM...
FLIP!
UH...HELLO?
FLIP!
OH!
YOU GOT UP JUST IN TIME!
BREAKFAST IS ALMOST READY.
UM-
SPEAKING OF, YOU WERE AN AWFUL FRIGHT WHEN I FOUND YOU LAST NIGHT.
YEAH..?
PLEASE, SIT AND HAVE BITE BEFORE IT GETS COLD!
BOING
BOING

YES! YOU WERE PRACTICALLY A CATSICLE. LUCKILY I WAS ON MY WAY HOME AND SPOTTED YOU OUT THERE, IT'S A MIRACLE YOU DIDN'T HAVE FROSTBITE.
FLIP!
...I SEE. THANK YOU, MR.?
BON APPÉTIT!
-BALTHIS, DOCTOR BALTHIS. BUT VIKTOR'S FINE, TOO.
DROOOOL...
TINK
MUNCH! MUNCH GULP
BUUUURP! CRUNCH
AH! HUNGRY, AREN'T WE?
MHM.
SO, DO TELL- HOW DID YOU END UP IN THE ELEMENTS, MISTER ELI?
IT WAS ON YOUR SHIRT TAG. (AND UNDERWEAR.)
YOU KNOW MY NAME..?
BUT STILL... I CAN'T IMAGINE YOU WERE EXPECTING TO GET ANYWHERE IN THIS WEATHER. WHAT COULD HAVE BEEN SO DIRE?
HM..VISITING A SICK RELATIVE PERHAPS?
WHERE ARE MY CLOTHES?
I DON'T GET MANY VISITORS OTHER THAN MY PATIENTS OUT HERE, SO I RELISH THE OPPORTUNITY TO GET TO KNOW SUCH AN INTRUIGING CHARACTER-
ALRIGHT, ENOUGH OF THIS BULLSHIT. I'M GRATEFUL THAT YA' HELPED ME BUT I DON'T APPRECIATE THE CROSS-EXAMINATION. I'M GONNA' FINISH EATING, GRAB MY THINGS AND I'LL BE OUT OF YER FUR, CAPISCE?
WHERE.
ARE.
MY.
CLOTHES?!

SIGH
YOU'RE NOT A VERY TALKATIVE FELLOW, ARE YOU?
SQUEAK.
YOUR CLOTHES ARE IN THE DRYER. THEY WERE SOAKED AND YOU WERE LOSING HEAT.
THERE, WAS THAT SO HARD?
HMPH.
...NO. BUT SPEAKING OF...
PAT.
SMUSH.
!!!
YOU BASTARD!!!
...IF I HAD TO STROLL ABOUT WITH THIS CUMBERSOME THING SWINGING AROUND I'D BE IRATE, TOO.
CLATTER!
GRIP.
THE LAUNDRY'S TWO DOORS DOWN. ON THE RIGHT.
HA HA HA HA!
FUCKING FREAK.
TMP
TMP
TMP
SQUINT.

FWOOOOOOOO...oo...
UNFORTUNATE, ISN'T IT?
IT LOOKS LIKE WE'RE SNOWED IN! IT'S FANTASTICAL IN A WAY. WHAT SAY YOU?
SMUSH!
ERGH...!
SQUEEK!
SUCH IS LIFE IN THE MOUNTAINS, EH? PERHAPS THE SUN WILL FREE US TOMORROW?
SERIOUSLY?!
HMM... THAT SURE IS A PERSISTENT PROBLEM, ISN'T IT?
DRIP
DROP
GRR...YA' KNOW WHAT?!
FLOP!
WHY SHOULD I FEEL ANY SHAME IN FRONT OF YOU?!
MY OH-MY!
AND IT'S NOT L-LIKE I'M ACTUALLY....
H-HORNY...
IT'S BEEN LIKE THIS AS LONG AS I CAN REMEMBER. IT WON'T GO AWAY UNLESS I "TAKE CARE OF IT", SO-
THEN DO IT.

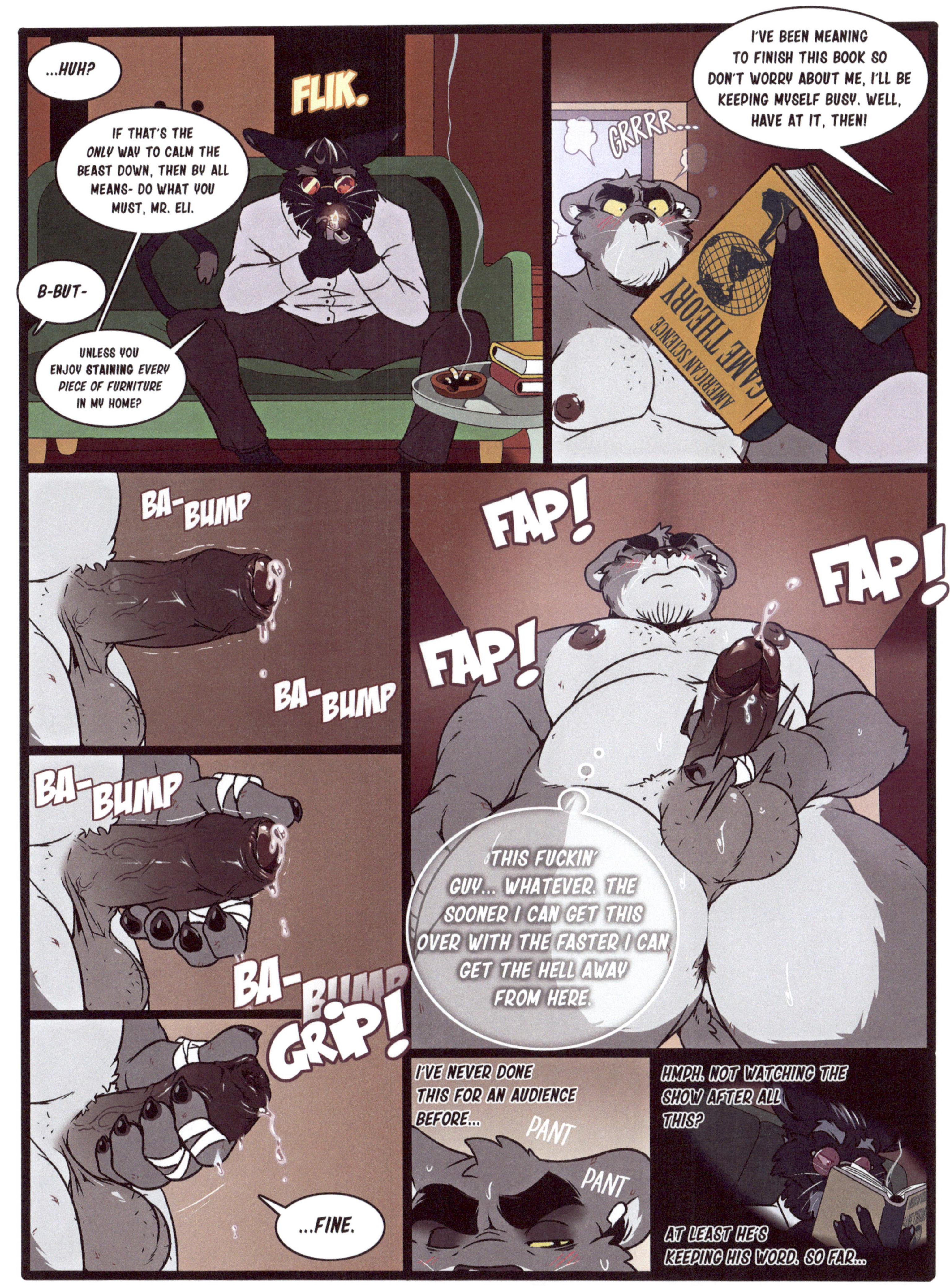

...HUH?
FLIK.
IF THAT'S THE ONLY WAY TO CALM THE BEAST DOWN, THEN BY ALL MEANS- DO WHAT YOU MUST, MR. ELI.
B-BUT-
UNLESS YOU ENJOY STAINING EVERY PIECE OF FURNITURE IN MY HOME?
GRRRR....
I'VE BEEN MEANING TO FINISH THIS BOOK SO DON'T WORRY ABOUT ME, I'LL BE KEEPING MYSELF BUSY. WELL, HAVE AT IT, THEN!
AMERICAN SCIENCE
GAME THEORY
BA-BUMP
BA-BUMP
BA-BUMP
BA-BUMP GRIP!
FAP!
FAP!
FAP!
THIS FUCKIN' GUY... WHATEVER. THE SOONER I CAN GET THIS OVER WITH THE FASTER I CAN GET THE HELL AWAY FROM HERE.
...FINE.
I'VE NEVER DONE THIS FOR AN AUDIENCE BEFORE...
PANT
PANT
HMPH. NOT WATCHING THE SHOW AFTER ALL THIS?
AT LEAST HE'S KEEPING HIS WORD. SO FAR...

SIX MINUTES LATER...
FAP
FAP
FAP
THIS IS TAKING A LOT LONGER THAN ANTICIPATED...
S-SHUT IT!
AMERICAN SCIENCE GAME THEORY
DRIP.
IF I KNEW YOU'D WORK UP THIS MUCH OF A SWEAT I'D HAVE PUT A TOWEL DOWN.
L-LOOK!!! I'VE NEVER DONE IT STANDING UP BEFORE, OKAY?! CHRIST.
IT FEELS WRONG!!!
PANT
PANT
OH! BY ALL MEANS, THEN.
...
PAT
PAT
NUDGE.
'SCUSE ME...
MHM.
BUMP.
THEEEERE WE GO...
PAP!
PAP!
PAP!
PAP!
PAP!
PAP!
PAP!
PAP!
SHF.
H-HEY, WHAT ARE YA'-
MMM...
DRAG...
PINCH
A-AH!!

I-I'M GONNA BLOW!
-URP!
SPLORT!
SPLUT!
PLAP.
PLIP.
AAAAHHHH...
TWEAK!
GASP!
MR. ELI!...
AMERICAN
FUCK...I-I'VE NEVER...
PANT
PANT
...SHOT THAT MUCH...
O MEIN GOTT!
POUNCE!
HUH??
WHAT A YIELD! COLOR ME IMPRESSED!

I MEAN, IN ALL MY YEARS...
...OF PLEASING MYSELF IN THAT CHAIR, I'VE NEVER MANAGED TO HIT THE WALL!
WH- YOU KEEP TRACK OF THE DISTANCE?!
CHRIST.
YER A LITTLE FREAK, AREN'T YA? "DOCTOR..."
THAT DID FEEL REALLY GOOD, THOUGH...
I'VE JUST DECIDED- THIS IS PROOF ENOUGH.
WAG
WAG
WHAT THE HELL?
MR. ELI, I'D LIKE FOR YOU TO LIVE HERE WORK AS MY ASSISTANT! I'LL PAY YOU A FAIR WAGE, PROVIDE LODGINGS, FOOD...WHAT DO YOU SAY?
FROM THAT ANGLE... HE DOESN'T LOOK HALF BAD?
UH-OH.
TWITCH.
...LEMME GET DRESSED BEFORE I EVEN ADDRESS THAT BATSHIT IDEA.
...
YES, OF COURSE.

MAKE YOURSELF AT HOME.
HUFF
HUFF
FAP
FAP
FAP
FAP
FAP

...ESSENTIALLY, YOU'D BE DOING A LOT OF ORGANIZING. KEEPING TRACK OF APPOINTMENTS, NAMES, ECT. NOT THE MOST THRILLING WORK BUT IT COMES WITH FREE LODGINGS IN THE GUEST QUARTERS, AS WELL AS MY HOME COOKING!
...WHY ME?
CHNK!
PFF. PFF.
YOU SEE, I CAN NEVER SEEM TO KEEP ASSISTANTS. THE DRIVE OUT HERE IN THE MOUNTAINS IS A DEAL BREAKER FOR MOST. I'D REALLY MUCH PREFER THAT POSITION BE FILLED BY SOMEONE WHO COULD STAY HERE FULL-TIME.
I'M SURE YOU'LL NEED TIME TO CONSIDER IT. BUT IF YOU DO, I CAN SEND FOR YOUR THINGS! WHERE DID YOU COME FROM?
SANTA FE.
THERE'S NO REASON TO CALL ANYBODY, THOUGH. DOUBT SOMEONE WOULD BE CHECKIN' FOR ME.
CHNK!
COUGH
SIDES, YOU GOT A NICE WASHER N' DRYER SO I'LL JUST KEEP WEARING THIS.
NONSENSE!
UNLESS YOU LIKE HOW THE BREEZE FEELS ON YOUR BARE-
WE'LL GO INTO TOWN SOMETIME AND BUY YOU A NEW WARDROBE. AND PERHAPS SOME BETTER FITTING PANTS?
FLIP!
PAF!
I'LL FIND A BELT.

. . .
OKAY. I'LL TAKE IT.
SPLENDID!
THE NEXT PATIENT ISN'T DUE UNTIL NEXT WEEK BUT YOU'LL BE PAID FOR YOUR TIME ANYWAY—
HEY.
WHIFF!
THE NEXT TIME YA' TOUCH ME WITHOUT MY PERMISSION...
... I'LL KNOCK YER FUCKIN' BLOCK OFF, GOT IT?
OH ELI, MY DEAR. THE NEXT TIME THAT I TOUCH YOU...
...WILL BE BECAUSE YOU WANT ME TO.
COME ALONG, THEN! IT'S LUNCH TIME.
ALRIGHT...

LATER THAT NIGHT...
DOC HAD ME ON MY FEET UNTIL SUNDOWN...
HMPH. AT LEAST I HAVE SOMEWHERE TO LAY LOW FOR AWHILE.
I'M BEAT...
THE NEXT TIME THAT I TOUCH YOU...,
...WILL BE BECAUSE YOU WANT ME TO.
HMM...
I MADE SURE TO LOCK IT.
BUT...
SCRAAAAAPE....
...CAN'T BE TOO CAREFUL.
FAP
FAP FAP

THEY'RE FOR ME..?
OF COURSE! I SAID I'D BUY YOU A NEW WARDDROBE, DIDN'T I?
I'M FAIRLY CERTAIN I GOT THE SIZING RIGHT...
...EXCEPT ON THE PANTS. COULD YOU TRY THEM ON FIRST?
HUH, ALRIGHT.
BAUDE
THEY'RE A BIT SNUG...
SHFFF...
RRGGHH!!!
SHIT!
SIGH WELL, AT LEAST YOU WON'T NEED A BELT.

OVER THE NEXT COUPLE OF DAYS I LEARNED MY NEW 'DUTIES' AS VIKTOR'S ASSISTANT.
...I WAS NOT EXPECTING TO DO THIS MUCH WRITING.
ASIDE FROM TIDYING UP AROUND THE PROPERTY, I WAS PUT IN CHARGE OF RECORD-KEEPNG, ORGANIZING PATIENT FILES AND ANY OTHER ODD-JOB VIK WAS TOO LAZY TO DO HIMSELF.
NORMALLY, DOING BASIC OFFICE WORK WOULD DRIVE ME CRAZY, BUT VIK KEEPS THINGS LIVELY. HE'S ALWAYS COOKING SOMETHING REALLY TASTY, TOO, WHICH MAKES SHARING MEALS TOGETHER A LITTLE LESS AWKWARD.
HE KEPT TRUE TO HIS WORD, TOO.
AFTER THAT FIRST DAY, HE NEVER TRIED TO TOUCH ME AGAIN.
BEFORE I KNEW IT, A WEEK HAD PASSED, AND HIS NEXT PATIENT WAS DUE TO ARRIVE IN THE AFTERNOON.
HE WANTS ME THERE TO RECORD THE SESSION, BUT I'M NOT SURE I'M QUALIFIED FOR THAT...

VERONICA MINX- THE FIRST PATIENT I'D ACTUALLY SEEN IN THE FLESH- ARRIVED IN THE AFTERNOON.
SORRY FOR BEING LATE!
...SHE WAS LATE.
SHE WAS ALSO BEAUTIFUL.
NO WORRIES! PLEASE, THIS WAY.
THANK YOU...
TICK.
I EXPECTED HIS PATIENTS TO MAINLY CONSIST OF OLD CRONES LOOKING FOR CHEAP MEDS.
SO, TELL ME WHY YOU'RE HERE TODAY.
TIK.
W-WELL...
THINGS HAVE BEEN HARD EVER SINCE MY LATE HUSBAND PASSED. I'VE FELT RESTLESS.
AH, MY CONDOLENCES.
TIK.
URGES, HM?
YES...WHILE I MISS HIM DEARLY, THERE'S A SORT OF...EXCITEMENT I FEEL BEING A SINGLE WOMAN ONCE AGAIN.
THANK YOU. BUT, YES...I DON'T KNOW WHAT TO DO WITH THESE STRANGE...URGES.
TIK.
TIK.
TIK.
LET'S SEE... WHAT WOULD SHE BE FILED UNDER?
I KNOW IT'S UNBECOMING OF A NEWLY WIDOWED WOMAN, BUT I FIND MYSELF CRAVING MEN. I STAY UP ALL NIGHT, DESPERATE FOR A STRONG, SUPPLE MAN TO COME AND-- OH, DOCTOR!!!
MISS VERONICA, I ASSURE YOU THESE ARE NORMAL THOUGHTS!
TICK!
PERHAPS...
RUSTLE
...YOU CAN HELP ME WORK THROUGH THEM, DOCTOR?
TICK!
OH MY...
ELI, WOULD YOU BE A DEAR AND GIVE ME A HAND, HERE?
ERK!
UM...VIK?
TICK!
TICK!

OH, YES!
PLEASE ME, MR.ELI!
WHAT THE FU-
POP!
HAVE YOU LOST YOUR MIND, LADY?!
H-HEY...
TICK.
FL OP!
Y-YOU'RE SERIOUS, HUH..?
MMM...WHAT A LOVELY SIZE...
TICK.
LICK...
TICK.
THIS IS FUCKING CRAZY! BUT... I HAVE BEEN REALLY PENT UP.

-BA-
BUMP!
MMPPPHHHH..!
A-AHH..
GLUK
GLUK
GLUK
MMM...
Y-YOU'RE REALLY GOOD AT THIS...
SLURP!
SCHLORP! MFF!
HORK SH
OH, YEAH! SHLUCK!
ZIMP!
FWOO-
RIGHTY-O, MR.ELI!
YOUR PERFORMANCE IS CERTAINLY EFFECTIVE ON MY END! PLEASE, KEEP UP THE GOOD WORK.
TICK!
TICK!
FINE, THEN.
HMPH. I SEE HOW IT IS, NOW...
FWIP-
SO THIS IS YOUR BIG GAME, DOCTOR?
I'LL SHOW YOU HOW IT'S DONE.

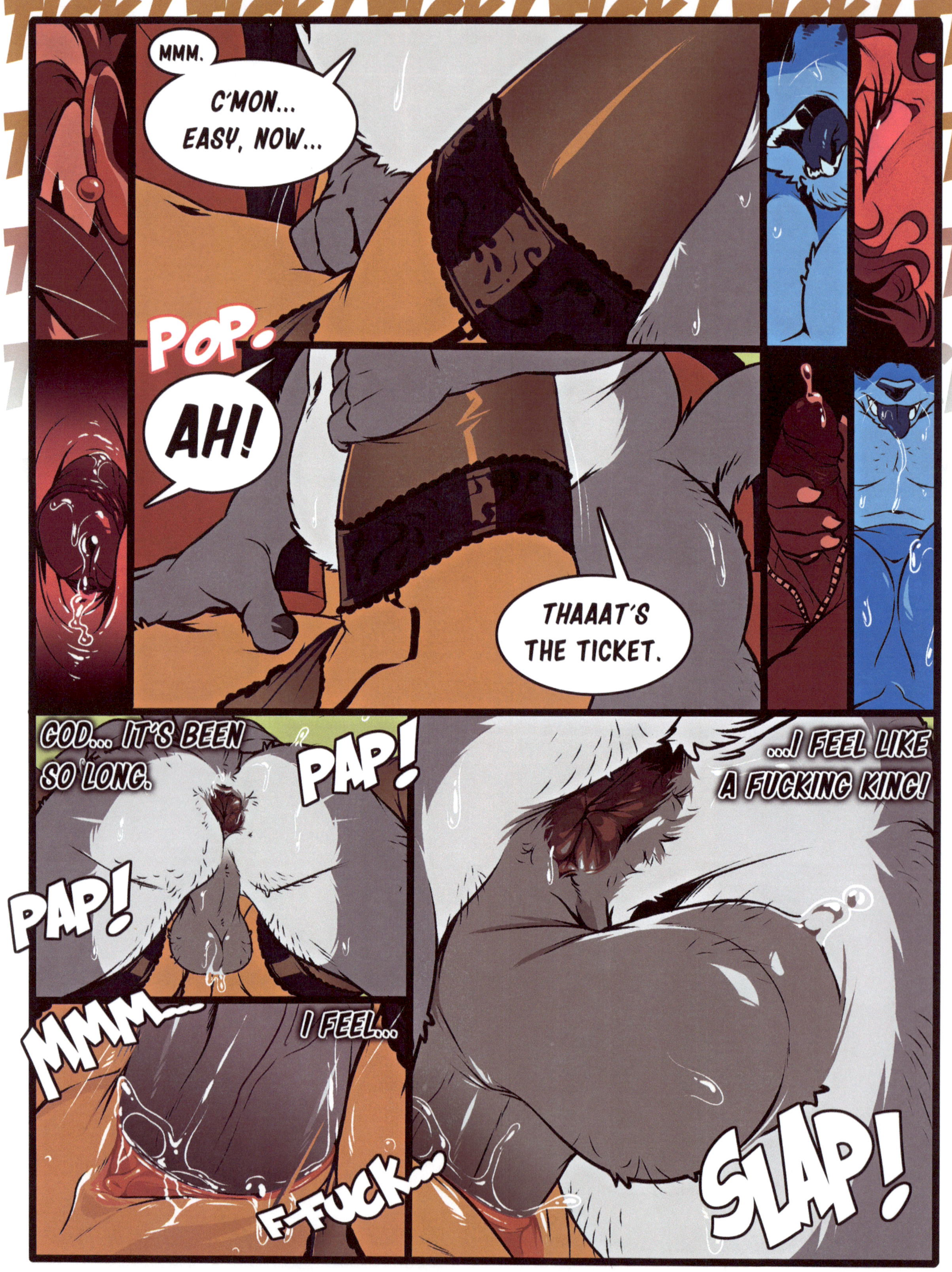

MMM.
C'MON... EASY, NOW...
POP.
AH!
THAAAT'S THE TICKET.
GOD... IT'S BEEN SO LONG.
PAP!
PAP!
...I FEEL LIKE A FUCKING KING!
MMM...
I FEEL...
F-FUCK...
SLAP!
TICK! TICK! TICK! TICK! TICK! T

MY, SHE IS GOOD...
BLINK.
WH-
WHAT THE FUCK ARE YOU DOING?!
GLUK
GLUK
HM?
THRUST!
THRUST!
YOU SEEMED QUITE ENRAPTURED BY HER, SO...
I WANTED A PIECE!
YOU SLY MOTHERFU-
PANT
JUST...STAY OUT OF MY WAY, OKAY?
PANT
AS YOU WISH, MR. ELI!
GLK!
GLK!
PAP!
PAP!
PAP!
MM...I'M GETTING RATHER CLOSE, DEAR.
TWITCH!
DEAR..?
I-I'M GETTING THERE...I JUST... N-NEED...

EIGHT MINUTES LATER...
SLAP!SLAP!SLAP!SLAP!SLAP!SL
P!SLAP!SL
P!SLAP!S
F-FUCK!!!
I ALMOST GOT THERE...AGAIN.
PANT
PANT
PANT
. . .
PANT
I WANT YOU TO TOUCH
HMM?
I DIDN'T QUITE CATCH THAT, ELI.
PANT
PANT
GRR!!!
I W-WA... WANT...
THIS FUCKING GUY...
I WANT YOU TO TOUCH MY CHEST AGAIN...
FLOP.
FLOP.
JIGGLE.
FLOP.
J-JUST...
DON'T MAKE IT W-WEIRD, OKAY?! I NEED TO CUM.
if you insist .
PINCH!
AH-!!

I-IF YOU KEEP PULLING LIKE THAT I-I'LL- MM!
TWITCH!
I...
YANK!
AH!
T-THATS...
DRIP.
DRIP.
SPLORT!
GAH!!!
GOOD SHOW!
SPLUT!
POP!
HRK!
ALLOW ME TO JOIN YOU!
MMM...
PANT
PANT
PANT
HEY, DOC- BE CAREFUL...
E-ELI?
GRAB
SQUISH...
EVERYTHING'S ALL SLIPPERY, YA' KNOW?
Y-YES... OF COURSE!

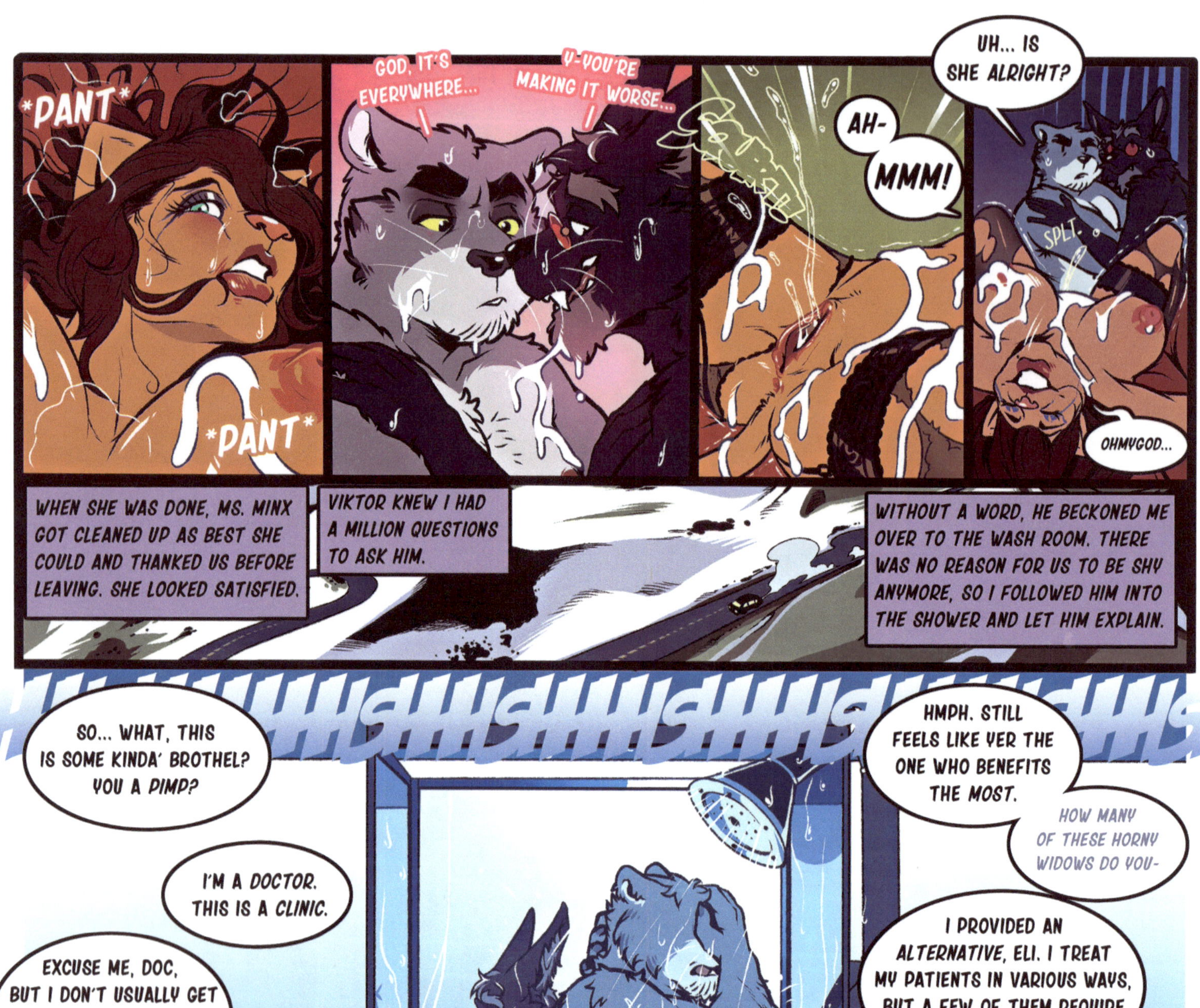

PANT
PANT
GOD, IT'S EVERYWHERE...
Y-YOU'RE MAKING IT WORSE...
AH-MMM!
UH... IS SHE ALRIGHT?
SPLT.
OHMYGOD...
WHEN SHE WAS DONE, MS. MINX GOT CLEANED UP AS BEST SHE COULD AND THANKED US BEFORE LEAVING. SHE LOOKED SATISFIED.
VIKTOR KNEW I HAD A MILLION QUESTIONS TO ASK HIM.
WITHOUT A WORD, HE BECKONED ME OVER TO THE WASH ROOM. THERE WAS NO REASON FOR US TO BE SHY ANYMORE, SO I FOLLOWED HIM INTO THE SHOWER AND LET HIM EXPLAIN.
SO... WHAT, THIS IS SOME KINDA' BROTHEL? YOU A PIMP?
I'M A DOCTOR. THIS IS A CLINIC.
EXCUSE ME, DOC, BUT I DON'T USUALLY GET MY BALLS DRAINED DURING A CHECK-UP. DON'T LIE TO ME.
I'M NOT LYING!
I'M A PSYCHIATRIST. MS. MINX... IS WHAT WE'D CALL A NYMPHOMANIAC. SHE CAN'T HELP BUT SEEK AN OUTLET FOR HER SEXUAL DESIRES. DO YOU KNOW WHAT THEY DO TO WOMEN LIKE HER, ELI?
UH... FUCK HER?
THEY'D SEND HER TO SOME POORLY-FUNDED SANITORIUM AND PUMP HER FULL OF DRUGS, TORTURE HER WITH ELECTRICITY... SHE'D HAVE NO FUTURE.
HMPH. STILL FEELS LIKE YER THE ONE WHO BENEFITS THE MOST.
HOW MANY OF THESE HORNY WIDOWS DO YOU-
I PROVIDED AN ALTERNATIVE, ELI. I TREAT MY PATIENTS IN VARIOUS WAYS, BUT A FEW OF THEM REQUIRE THIS INTENSIVE CARE.
...WHY INVOLE ME?
MM. YOU POSSESS A STAGGERING LEVEL OF SEXUAL-ENERGY... AND ARE EASY ON THE EYES.
HMPH. WELL, I'M FLATTERED, BUT YOU'RE STILL WEIRD.
I CAN LIVE WITH THAT, ELI! HA-HA!

PLIP.
HOWEVER...
...IT DIDN'T TAKE MUCH TO CONVINCE YOU, MR. ELI.
PLIP.
PLIP.
CAREFUL, DOC.
I AIN'T YER PLAY-THING.
YER FORGETTING ONE VERY IMPORTANT FACTOR HERE.
DO ENLIGHTEN ME.
SQUEEEZE
I'M BIGGER THAN YOU.
STRONGER THAN YOU.
IF I FELT LIKE TURNING THIS LITTLE GAME AROUND...
...I COULD DO ANYTHING I WANTED TO YOUR BODY.
GRIND...
YES, BUT...
YOU WON'T.
BLINK.
HMPH.
I S'POSE YER RIGHT...
H-HEY...
OR RATHER: YOU CAN'T.
FLOP.
GRAB

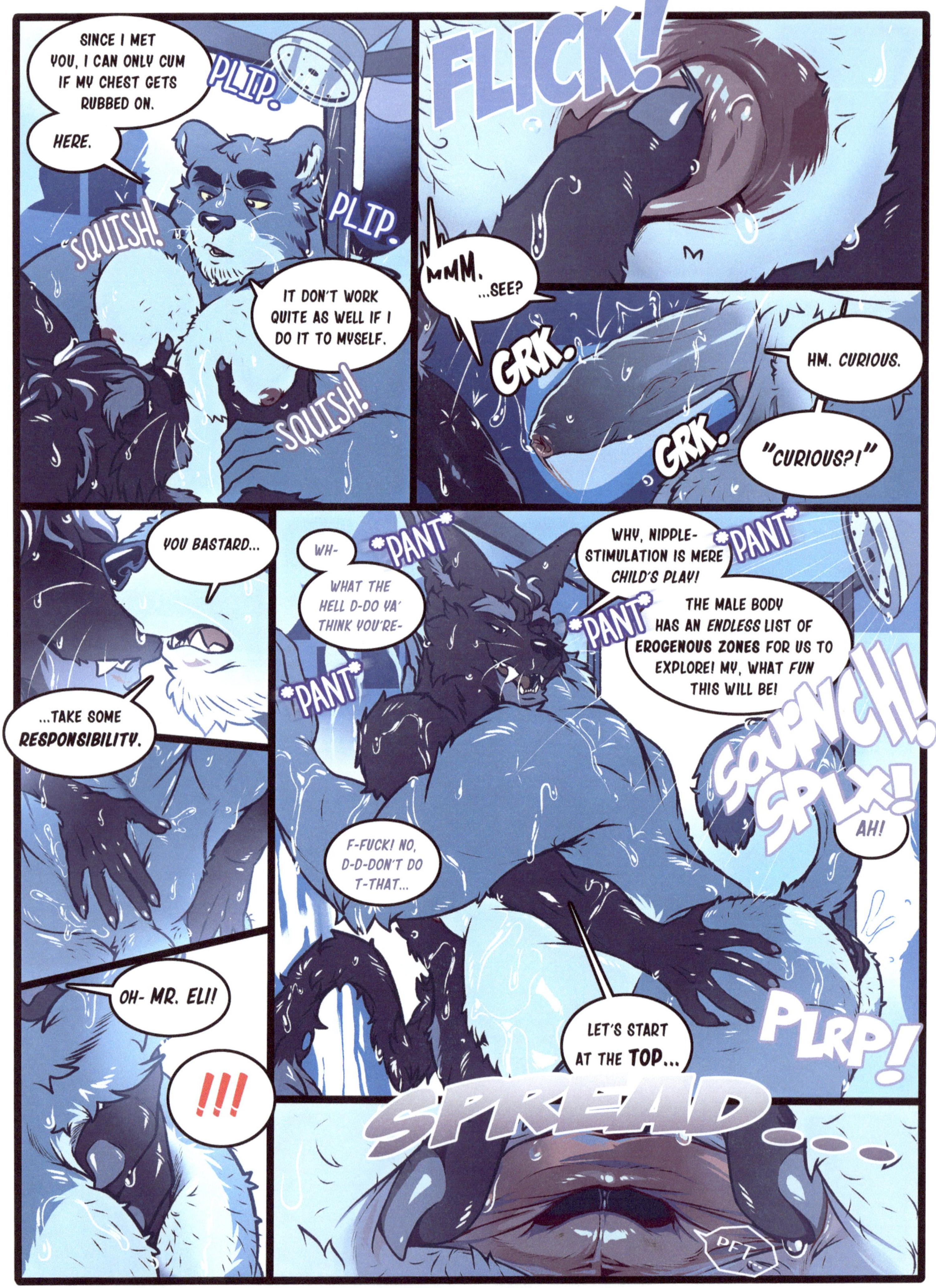

SINCE I MET YOU, I CAN ONLY CUM IF MY CHEST GETS RUBBED ON.
HERE.
PLIP.
PLIP.
SQUISH!
SQUISH!
IT DON'T WORK QUITE AS WELL IF I DO IT TO MYSELF.
FLICK!
MMM.
...SEE?
GRK.
GRK.
HM. CURIOUS.
"CURIOUS?!"
YOU BASTARD...
...TAKE SOME RESPONSIBILITY.
OH- MR. ELI!
!!!
WH- WHAT THE HELL D-DO YA' THINK YOU'RE-
PANT
PANT
PANT
F-FUCK! NO, D-D-DON'T DO T-THAT...
WHY, NIPPLE-STIMULATION IS MERE CHILD'S PLAY!
THE MALE BODY HAS AN ENDLESS LIST OF EROGENOUS ZONES FOR US TO EXPLORE! MY, WHAT FUN THIS WILL BE!
PANT
PANT
SQUNCH!
SPLX!
AH!
LET'S START AT THE TOP...
PLRP!
SPREAD...

STOP.
TWITCH.
EH?
STOP TOUCHING ME THERE.
A-HA...
MY BOY, IF IT'S HYGIENE YOU'RE WORRIED ABOUT, WE'RE ALREADY IN THE SHOWER, SO-
I... SAID... STOP!!!
WHAM!
SQUIK
F-FINE. NO MORE...
IT S-SEEMS SOME BOUNDARIES NEED TO BE SET.
. . .
BUT... PLEASE DON'T LEAVE. STAY HERE WITH ME.
LEAVE..?
TCH...
YOU ASSHOLE. AS IF I COULD LEAVE...
...WHEN I'VE BEEN GIVEN SUCH AN EASY GIG.

...AND SO, THINGS CONTINUED ON AS USUAL. I KEPT ON FUCKING THE PATIENTS HE DEEMED TO NEED OUR SPECIAL TREATMENT.
EVERY GIRL WAS MORE ATTRACTIVE THAN THE LAST. I WAS STARTING TO THINK HE JUST HIRED HOOKERS OFF THE STREET.
THE GOOD DOCTOR WOULD USUALLY JUST WATCH. I DUNNO WHY, BUT I FELT MORE COMFORTABLE WITH HIM BEING THERE.
PANT FUCK ME... DADDY... *PANT*
PANT I'M YOUR... LITTLE GIRL...
BUT EVERY NOW AND THEN, THEY'D SAY SOMETHING A LITTLE OFF. CAN'T PUT MY FINGER ON IT.
PAP!
PAP!
GRIND...
OOUGH! AHH...
AND LIKE CLOCKWORK, THE ISSUE OF EXHAUSTION WOULD REAR ITS UGLY HEAD...
FLOP.
FLOP.
YOU'RE DOING GREAT, CHAMP.
WHUH..?
PLOP.

AHH- SLAP! TWEAK. TWEAK.
THAT'S THE TICKET...
SLAP!
PINCH.
SLAP! SLAP!
THERE WE GO! THAT WASN'T SO HARD, WAS IT, ELI?
HEY!
LIFT.
PAP.
GOODNESS- JUST LOOK AT HOW IT FLEXES WITH EACH PUMP!
PAP.
TWITCH.
TWITCH.
PAP.
MMMMM...
SPLORT!
FLOP!
MR. ELI... IT SEEMS OUR PATIENT IS IN NEED OF FURTHER TREATMENT.
AH... P-PLEASE...
HUH? BUT I-
DON'T STOP...
YES, YOU MAY HAVE ACHEIVED ORGASM, BUT THE MADAME HERE HAS YET TO CLIMAX.
SLUP.
I'LL TAKE CARE OF IT.
HE'S EATING MY-?!
SLURRRRP. SUCK. SUCK.
...DAMMIT.
J-JESUS-
LICK.
WHAT THE FUCK IS HE DOING?!
SMACK!
OUGHH...
LAP!
LAP!
NGHHH!
LAP!

ZIP.
IT'S MY TURN.
AH-!!
OH, THAT'S VERRRY SLICK...
MMM...
EASY, DEAR.
PLAP!
PLAP!
PLAP!
ELI, YOU DID A MARVELOUS JOB OF WARMING HER UP!
!
HMPH.
CAN'T LET YA' HAVE ALL THE FUN, DOC. I'LL TAKE THIS SIDE FOR A SPIN.
PLP
HAH...
GLUK
MMF!
GLUK
MMM...
I CAN GET USED TO THIS...
IT'S RIGHT IN FRONT OF ME...
PLAP...
PLAP...
SLOW-MOTION CAM

YIPE!
PANT
PANT
HIS BREATH KINDA TICKLES...
SNIFF
SNIFF
WAIT- NO! DAMN IT.
GOODNESS... THAT AROMA!
BAD THOUGHTS!
I CAN FEEL THE GLARE OF A PREDATOR STARING STRAIGHT AT MY ASS!
UGH... HOW GROSS. WHAT KIND OF CAT WANTS A FACE-FULL OF A MAN'S ASS?!
OI.
YOU CAN LOOK, BUT DON'T TOUCH, DOC.
...
PFT! THAT FACE!
WAIT... DO I ACTUALLY HAVE CONTROL HERE?
SIGH FINE... BUT ONLY WHEN YER ABOUT TO CUM.
HUFF
SLAP!
SLAP!
HUFF
GAH!!
PAP!
PAP!
UGH... THIS IS TAKING TOO LONG!
MMM... GOOD BOY.
...I'M WEAK.
HAHHH...
DOC?!

GONNA-!
PAP
PAP!
SPLURT!
W-WHY YOU LITTLE...
HUFF...
HUFF...
GODS... HIS SCENT IS STRONG... IF ONLY I COULD TASTE IT...
YOU KNOW I'M GONNA CLOBBER YA' LATER, RIGHT?
FUCKING FREAK...
HUFF
HUFF
SNIIIIIFFFFF...
WORTH IT.
ALRIGHT...
ALRIGHT!
POP!
WH-?!
YOU'VE FINISHED, SO GET YOUR FACE OUTTA' MY-
SPLAT!
AH...
SO THAT'S HOW IT IS...
MY WORST FEARS CAME INTO LIGHT AT THAT VERY MOMENT.
SMACK!

I'M GONNA TAKE A QUICK SHOWER BEFORE BED, SO...
CREAK...
...G'NIGHT, VIKTOR.
GOODNIGHT...
SLAM!
FWUMP.
FINALLY... UGH, I'M STILL NOT USED TO BEIN' STICKY ALL THE TIME.
WHATEVER. AT LEAST I HAVE THE SHOWER ALL TO MYSELF THIS TIME.
HMM...
DA-DUM...
SQUEAK.
SQUEAK!
I STILL CAN'T BELIEVE DOC NUTTED FROM SMELLIN' MY ASS... WHAT A FREAK.
IT'S A MAN'S MOST PRIVATE PLACE, YA' KNOW?!
SWIPE.
...JUST A QUICK CHECK.
SNIFF
SNIFF
YUCK!
YEP- IT SMELLS LIKE ASS.
CLEAN.
CLEAN...
CLEAN!!!

AHH... THAT'S SO MUCH BETTER.
IT'S BEEN AWHILE SINCE I TOOK A GOOD HARD LOOK AT MYSELF IN THE MIRROR
I'M GETTING OLD. WELL, OLDER.
....YEP, ALL CLEAN.
WHAT THE HELL IS SO GREAT ABOUT MY ASS, ANYWAY?
AND THEN HE FOUND A MIRROR.
CHRIST, I CAN BARELY SEE ANYTHING PAST MY GUT.
I'VE NEVER ACTUALLY TAKEN A GOOD LOOK AT IT BEFORE...
IT'S SO... SO...
...PINK.

STILL, FROM THIS ANGLE IT'S HARD TO REALLY SEE MUCH...
HUH...WHEN YOU SPREAD IT LIKE THIS, IT LOOKS A LOT TIGHTER.
MMM...
KINDA SMALL COMPARED TO THE SIZE OF MY ASS CHEEKS.
OOPS... LOOKS LIKE A LITTLE WATER MANAGED TO GET TRAPPED IN THERE. I DID WASH IT PRETTY HARD.
DRIP.
THE MORE I TOUCH AND MESS WITH IT, THE SOFTER IT GETS.
LIKE A WOMAN'S...
CHRIST, I CAN ALMOST SEE WHAT I ATE FOR LUNCH!
DID I MANAGE TO BREAK SOMETHING?!
HUP!
MAYBE IF I TRY FROM THIS ANGLE...
PHEW. IT WENT BACK TO A LITTLE PUCKER.
...
GOD THIS IS EMBARRASSING...
WILL IT-
O-OH! YEAHHH...
FUCK!!!

HUFF
HUFF
FUCK!

POP!
AH!
SNIFF SNIFF.
IT SMELLS...
...LIKE ASS.
MMMF...
I DON'T KNOW WHAT'D COME OVER ME THAT NIGHT, BUT I COULDN'T STOP MYSELF. IT FELT LIKE A NEW DOOR HAD BEEN OPENED.
MAYBE IT WAS A DOOR THAT SHOULD HAVE STAYED SHUT. WHO'S TO SAY?
IS THIS WHAT DOC WANTED ALL ALONG?
BEFORE I KNEW IT, SPRING HAD ARRIVED IN THE MOUNTAINS. THE SNOW MELTED TO GIVE WAY TO PATCHES OF GREEN.
THE OPPRESSIVE WALL OF ICE HAD KEPT ME PRISONER HERE WAS GONE. I SHOULD FEEL RELIEVED, BUT...
...I'VE GROWN COMFY LIVING HERE WITH HIM.
FEELS LIKE JUST YESTERDAY THAT WE MET, EH DOC?
YES... THIS WINTER WAS RATHER SHORT. I THOUGHT WE'D HAVE MORE...
...NO. THIS IS GOOD.

HUH..?
I SUPPOSE...
...YOU'RE LIKELY READY TO RETURN TO YOUR OLD LIFE NOW.
MAYBE IT WAS A LITTLE VACATION FOR YOU, OR A NICE LONG DREAM.
ONE WE SHARED.
AFTER ALL, YOU NEVER HAD A CHOICE IN THE MATTER. I-
BLINK.
I STAYED BECAUSE I WANTED TO. I LIKE LIVIN' HERE WITH YOU. AND...
YOU'RE WRONG.
...WELL, WHATEVER YOU WANT TO CALL IT, WE'RE TOGETHER NOW. I'M PART OF THE TEAM, GOT IT?
IT FEELS LIKE I'D ALWAYS BEEN HERE- BY HIS SIDE. I CAN'T IMAGINE LIFE WITHOUT HIM ANYMORE...
DOES THAT MEAN..?
MY APOLOGIES. I SHOULD HAVE NEVER DOUBTED YOU.
SHALL WE TIDY UP THE YARD?
...OF COURSE.
YES SIR!

OH-MY!
IT'S CERTAINLY BECOME QUITE WARM OUTSIDE, EH, ELI?
EE-YUP.
ZZZ!!!
I DON'T ENVY YOU, SLAVING AWAY IN THIS HEAT. THOUGH IT'S LOVELY FROM WHERE I'M SITTING.
YES, INDEED...
EE-YUP.
DING.
...IT'S GOOD TO BE KING.
POLO
WHAT THE HELL IS HIS PROBLEM TODAY..?
GRR...
WAIT... IS HE TRYING TO BAIT ME BY GETTING ME ANGRY?
ALRIGHT, VIK.
SNAP!
LET'S PLAY!
WHOOPS!
SOME KING, BUYIN' ME ALL THESE CHEAP CLOTHES...
WHOOOOSH...
HE... WASN'T EVEN LOOKING AT ME?!
SHFF
OH. IT'S JUST HIS STUPID HAT.
OOP.

FWIP.
A-ANYWAY...
ALL OF THIS HARD WORK'S GOT ME NEEDIN' TO TAKE A LEAK SOMETHIN' FIERCE.
I DON'T THINK I CAN MAKE IT BACK TO THE HOUSE IN TIME!
WHAT TO DO..?
GUESS I'LL HAVE TO DO MY BUSINESS RIGHT HERE.
YOU MIND?
SHFF...
C'MON, I KNOW YOU CAN'T TAKE YOUR EYES OFF THIS FAT ASS.
TOO STUNNED TO SPEAK, EH? THAT'S A FIRST.
...
THAT'S OK. AFTER ALL, WE'RE THE ONLY ONES AROUND HERE FOR MILES AND-
HOWDY, DR. BALTHIS!
POOF!
AM...
...I INTERRUPTING SOMETHING, SIR?

AH... SO YOU'RE HERE TO DELIVER SOME MAIL TO VIKTOR?
INDEED. THE SNOW WAS FAR TOO DEEP FOR THE POST OFFICE TO SEND ANY PERSONNEL OUT THIS WAY.
SORRY...
I MEANT TO CALL AHEAD OF TIME, BUT THINGS JUST GOT HECTIC AT THE CENTER.
THIS GUY'S JUST A KID... YET HE'S TALKING TO VIK LIKE THEY'RE FRIENDS.
LET'S SEE...
SOME BILLS... A FEW BANK STATE-MENTS... OH! AND A POSTCARD!
NOW THAT I THINK ABOUT IT, JUST HOW FAR AWAY FROM TOWN ARE WE OUT HERE?
I CAN'T REMEMBER ANYTHING ABOUT THE NIGHT I ARRIVED HERE.
VERNON, I'LL BE SURE TO SEND MY REGARDS TO YOUR SUPERIORS AND TELL THEM YOU WENT ABOVE AND BEYOND TO DELIVER MY PRECIOUS MAIL IN SUCH A TIMELY MANNER!
WOO-HOO!
I HAVE A TIP FOR YOU, AS WELL...
GEEZ... I ALMOST FEEL SORRY FOR THE KID. I UNDERSTAND WHAT IT'S LIKE TO DO ANYTHING TO EARN A FEW BUCKS.
REALLY, THANK YOU, SIR...
I'M ONLY A HANDY-MAN, BUT THEY'VE BEGUN TO TRUST ME WITH MORE IMPORTANT TASKS AFTER YOUR LAST CALL! HOPEFULLY THEY'LL RAISE MY PAY...
SO YOU DON'T WORK AT THE POST-OFFICE, YOU JUST RUN ERRANDS IN TOWN?
PRETTY MUCH! I TAKE WHATEVER WORK I CAN, SIR. ANYTHING TO SAVE UP.
I WONDER IF VIK COULD OFFER HIM SOME WORK HERE AT THE HOUSE. WELL, NORMAL WORK.

WHAT ABOUT YER PARENTS, KID?
OH! WELL... I HAD A COLLEGE FUND, BUT THEY ENDED UP PUTTING ALL OF IT INTO A WAR BOND DURING KOREA... LET'S JUST SAY THEY DIDN'T MAKE ANY RETURNS ON THAT INVESTMENT, SO NOW IT'S UP TO ME TO PAY FOR MY SCHOOLING.
OH, IT'S FINE, REALLY.
YEESH... THAT'S ROUGH.
UM.
I'M JUST HAPPY TO BE OF USE TO SOMEONE.
VERNON IS FAR TOO KIND FOR HIS OWN GOOD.
SHFF.
HE'S MODEST, BUT DON'T BE FOOLED- HE'S GOT A BRILLIANT MIND WHEN IT COMES TO PROBLEM-SOLVING, ELI.
OH PLEASE! IT'S NOTHING LIKE THAT, SIR.
HMPH... WHY ARE THEY BEING SO BUDDY-BUDDY? WAIT, DID THIS KID ALREADY DO FOR VIK WHAT I'M DOING NOW..?
DING-DONG!
DING-DONG!
AH- I DO BELIEVE THAT IS TODAY'S CLIENT.
ELI, BE A DEAR AND KEEP OUR GUEST COMPANY-
WHAT?! BUT YOU DIDN'T MENTION A-
AH!
W-WELL, I'M SURE WE CAN GET ALONG JUST FINE!
STAY...
WITH VERNON?!
UM, WHERE ARE YOU GOING? CAN I COME ALONG?
OH...
SO, HOW DID YOU AND THE DOCTOR MEET-
SHE REQUESTED MY SERVICES ONLY, SO YOU AREN'T NEEDED TODAY, HA-HA!
TOODLES~!
WHILE HE GETS TO SCREW SOME BROAD WITHOUT ME?!
NEED TO PISS. AND NO.

PSSSSSSSSSSSS
SHEESH... VIKTOR'S OFF HIS ROCKER IF HE THINKS I'M GOING TO SPEND ALL DAY WITH THIS NEW KID INSTEAD OF FUCKIN'.
IT'S BEEN A WEEK SINCE OUR LAST SESSION...
...MY DICK'S ACHING FOR SOME ACTION.
BUMP.
PARDON ME, SIR.
HUH? OOPS.
WHAT THE HELL IS WITH THIS GUY?! THERE'S PLENTY OF OTHER PLACES TO TAKE A PISS AROUND HERE!
WHEW...
THAT LEMONADE WENT RIGHT THROUGH ME, HA-HA!
SSSSSSSS...
WHO CARES?! GO PISS SOMEWHERE ELSE!
UGH, WHATEVER.
SO LONG AS HE KEEPS HIS DISTANCE...

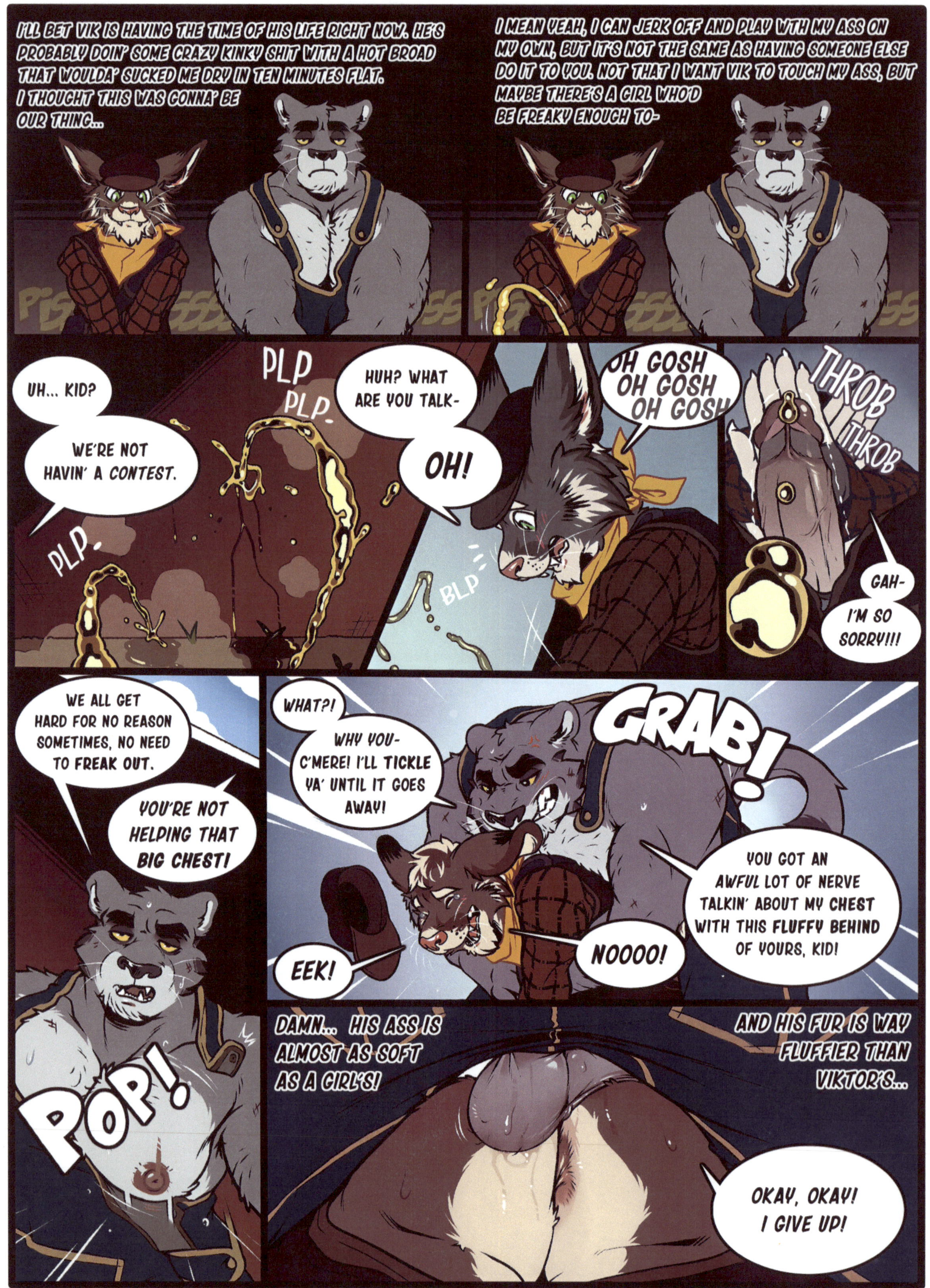

I'LL BET VIK IS HAVING THE TIME OF HIS LIFE RIGHT NOW. HE'S PROBABLY DOIN' SOME CRAZY KINKY SHIT WITH A HOT BROAD THAT WOULDA' SUCKED ME DRY IN TEN MINUTES FLAT. I THOUGHT THIS WAS GONNA' BE OUR THING...
I MEAN YEAH, I CAN JERK OFF AND PLAY WITH MY ASS ON MY OWN, BUT IT'S NOT THE SAME AS HAVING SOMEONE ELSE DO IT TO YOU. NOT THAT I WANT VIK TO TOUCH MY ASS, BUT MAYBE THERE'S A GIRL WHO'D BE FREAKY ENOUGH TO-
UH... KID?
WE'RE NOT HAVIN' A CONTEST.
PLP.
PLP.
PLP.
HUH? WHAT ARE YOU TALK-
OH!
OH GOSH OH GOSH OH GOSH
BLP.
THROB
THROB
GAH- I'M SO SORRY!!!
WE ALL GET HARD FOR NO REASON SOMETIMES, NO NEED TO FREAK OUT.
YOU'RE NOT HELPING THAT BIG CHEST!
WHAT?!
WHY YOU- C'MERE! I'LL TICKLE YA' UNTIL IT GOES AWAY!
GRAB!
EEK!
NOOOO!
YOU GOT AN AWFUL LOT OF NERVE TALKIN' ABOUT MY CHEST WITH THIS FLUFFY BEHIND OF YOURS, KID!
POP!
DAMN... HIS ASS IS ALMOST AS SOFT AS A GIRL'S!
AND HIS FUR IS WAY FLUFFIER THAN VIKTOR'S...
OKAY, OKAY! I GIVE UP!

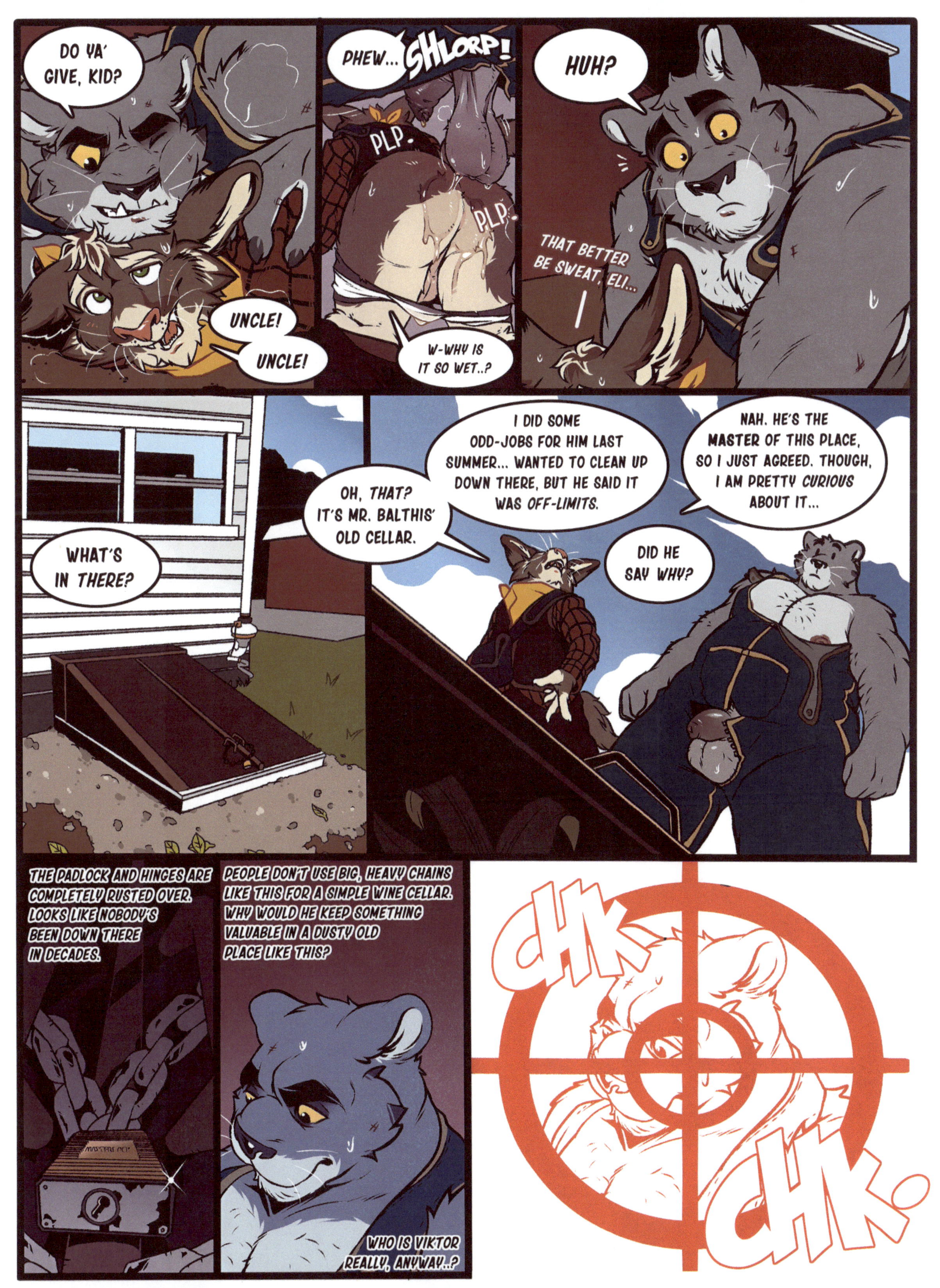

DO YA' GIVE, KID?
UNCLE!
UNCLE!
PHEW... SHLORP!
PLP.
PLP.
W-WHY IS IT SO WET..?
HUH?
THAT BETTER BE SWEAT, ELI...
WHAT'S IN THERE?
OH, THAT? IT'S MR. BALTHIS' OLD CELLAR.
I DID SOME ODD-JOBS FOR HIM LAST SUMMER... WANTED TO CLEAN UP DOWN THERE, BUT HE SAID IT WAS OFF-LIMITS.
DID HE SAY WHY?
NAH. HE'S THE MASTER OF THIS PLACE, SO I JUST AGREED. THOUGH, I AM PRETTY CURIOUS ABOUT IT...
THE PADLOCK AND HINGES ARE COMPLETELY RUSTED OVER. LOOKS LIKE NOBODY'S BEEN DOWN THERE IN DECADES.
PEOPLE DON'T USE BIG, HEAVY CHAINS LIKE THIS FOR A SIMPLE WINE CELLAR. WHY WOULD HE KEEP SOMETHING VALUABLE IN A DUSTY OLD PLACE LIKE THIS?
WHO IS VIKTOR REALLY, ANYWAY..?
CHK
CHK.

PANT
WH...
WHY...
WHY DID Y-YOU STOP..?
PANT
PANT
...APOLOGIES.
CLICK.
JUST SOME RATS IN THE GARDEN-- NOTHING TO WORRY ABOUT, DEAR.

HEY, UH...
WHY ARE WE BOTH GETTING NAKED?
FIRST REASON:
IT'S HOT AS HELL, AND WE'RE COVERED IN SWEAT.
SECOND, YOU NEED TO GET RID OF THAT HARD-ON.
O-OH...
POP.
DAMN.
DAMN.
DAMN.
DRIP
DRIP
I'M SORRY FOR MAKING THIS A WHOLE THING...
DON'T APOLOGIZE.
I... GOT A LITTLE EXCITED MYSELF. OOPS.
BO-YOING!
HEY...
YO, KID.

"HOW WOULD YOU LIKE TO MAKE SOME EXTRA MONEY?"

HUH..?
I D-DON'T KNOW WHAT YOU-
NO, IT'S PROBABLY JUST THE HEAT. YOU'RE TALKING NONSENSE!
NOPE.
THAT TIGHT LITTLE ASS HAS GOT ME ALL RILED UP, TOO. YOU'VE GOTTA' TAKE RESPONSIBILITY.
PAP
PAP
B-BUT I-
SPREAD IT.
WOULD... YOU SEEING MY ASS REALLY MAKE YOU THAT HAPPY, MR. ELI?
TREMENDOUSLY.
MY, MY...
I'D BE A FOOL TO REFUSE AN OFFER THAT GENEROUS!
SHFF.
SO... DOES IT LOOK OKAY, SIR?

Y-YEAH...
CAN YOU GET A GOOD VIEW LIKE THIS, MR. ELI?
MHM.
IT'S NOT VERY COMFORTABLE... MY ARMS ARE GETTING TIRED, SIR.
LESS TALKING, MORE SPREADIN', KID.
PFAPFAPFAP
PFAPFAPFAPFA
HAH...
HAH...
PFAPFAPFAP
TMP.
O-OH!
MMM... YOUR BREATH FEELS SO WARM BACK THERE, MR. ELI.
...
DO...
...YOU WANT TO TAKE A CLOSER LOOK, SIR?
PAP PAP

THIS CAN'T BE REAL... EVERYTHING ABOUT HIM IS IMPOSSIBLY SOFT. WARM...
HIS SMELL... IT'S SO INTOXICATING.
THAT'S IT-- I CAN'T RESIST IT ANY LONGER!!!
AH!
GOD, I CAN'T EVEN DESCRIBE IT.
HIS SMELL AND TASTE IS SO DIFFERENT FROM MY OWN... IT'S SO MUCH SWEETER. CLEANER. YOUNGER.
EVEN TOUCHING HIS DICK DOESN'T FEEL AS WEIRD AS I EXPECTED IT TO. IT'S SO EASY.
FUCK! DOC WAS RIGHT ALL ALONG!!!
DOC WAS RIGHT.
DOC WAS RIGHT.
OLD BASTARD!

GET ON TOP OF ME.
OKAY.
SQUISH
SHLP! PLP PLP
--AH! D-DEEPER...
KISSING ANOTHER MAN...
ALL OF THIS FEELS SO RIGHT... HE'S EXACTLY WHAT I WANTED.
Y-YOU CAN PUT IT IN ME, SIR.
PLEASE, HURRY UP...
SQUEEZE...
UM...
IS IT EVEN GOING TO FIT?!
GRIP!
GRIP!
FUCK IT, THERE'S NO GOING BACK, NOW.
SORRY, KID. THIS ASS IS ABOUT TO GET DESTROYED.

UM...
HEY, SIR?

HUH?

C-CAN I
STOP DOING THIS
POSE, NOW?

MY BACK IS REALLY
STARTING TO HURT...

...

YEAH...

SORRY.

THROB.

THROB.

UM... I'M
SORRY IF I DID SOME-
THING WRONG.

NO!

YOU DID
JUST FINE. I SHOULDN'T
HAVE ASKED YOU TO
DO THIS...

I DON'T MIND.

MMM...

LISTEN,
IT MAY HAVE
BEEN FUN...

BUT.

WE CAN NEVER TELL ANYONE ABOUT WHAT WE JUST DID.

HMM? NOW WHAT ARE YOU DOING IN HERE, ELI?
TRYING TO RECALL OUR LAST SESSION, PERHAPS? I DO APOLOGIZE FOR EXCLUDING YOU, BUT THIS PATIENT HAD VERY, UH... PARTICULAR INTERESTS. NOT YOUR SORT OF THING.
MHM.
OH, COME NOW! DON'T BE SO CROSS, THESE CASES ARE A RARITY!
HEY, DOC. CAN I... ASK YOU A QUESTION?
YES?
THE NIGHT IS STILL YOUNG!
WHAT ARE YOU IN THE MOOD FOR? BOARD GAMES? A PUZZLE?
HAS THERE EVER BEEN A TIME...
BLINK.
BLINK.
...BOY.
WHERE THE HELL DID THAT COME FROM? ARE YOU DRUNK?!
...WHEN YOU FELL IN LOVE WITH ONE OF YOUR PATIENTS?

YOINK.
...CURIOUS.
NOT AT ALL. I'M JUST FEELING A LITTLE...
ELI?!
TWITCH
TWITCH
WH-
WHAT THE-
EEEEEK!
HEY!!!
THIS J-JUST ISN'T LIKE YOU! I'M GETTING WORRIED!
ARE YOU FEELING ALRIGHT? DO YOU HAVE A HIGH TEMPERATURE?! PLEASE, TELL ME WHAT'S AILING YOU, MR. ELI!
C'MON! WHY'RE YOU ACTING SHY ALL OF A SUDDEN?!
I KNOW YOU'VE BEEN LOOKING AT ME, DOC. YOU KEEP FINDING EXCUSES TO GROPE ME AND SHIT WHILE WE'RE SCREWIN' THOSE BROADS. YOU ATE MY CUM!
SO TELL ME! ARE YOU INTO ME, OR IS IT A CHARADE?!
...
ANSWER ME!!!
SHIVER
SHIVER
DO.
YOU.
LIKE.
MEN?

HE ANSWERED ME . . .
. . . WITH A KISS .
AND
I
REPLIED.

MM...
MMM!
HAAAAAAAAHHH...
...OH?
YOUR CURIOUSITY KNOWS NO BOUNDS...
F-FUCK, A GIRL'S NEVER KISSED ME ALL AGGRESSIVE LIKE THIS...
HOWEVER, I SIMPLY MUST CORRECT YOU ON-
AH!
-ON YOUR SYNTAX, MY DEAR. MUST I SPELL IT OUT FOR YOU?
GRTLP.
WH-WHUH ARE YOU..?
IT'S NOT ABOUT MEN-
HUMP!
HUMP!
HUMP!
MMF!
-OR ABOUT WOMEN, OR EVEN MY PREFERENCE FOR ONE'S PARTS.
I SIMPLY...
...LIKE INTERESTING PEOPLE. THAT'S ALL.

AND YOU...
...ARE ONE HELL OF AN INTERESTING PERSON, ELI.
I DUNNO ABOUT THAT...
DRIP.
SHFF SHFF
MM... YOU SURE ABOUT THAT?
HNNNGGGG.... I J-JUST MEAN...
RUB RUB.
OKAY!
FINE.
I'M INTERESTING! NOW QUIT TEASIN' ME AND PUT IT-
HUH?
SWIF
OHHH NO,.. ELI, YOU'VE GOT IT ALL WRONG.
...OKAY?
DID YOU THINK I'D JUST SUBMIT TO YOU SO EASILY? REWARDS HAVE TO BE EARNED, BOY.
I'M THE BOSS.
POKE.
SIX WEEKS. I'LL GIVE YOU THAT LONG, ELI.
IN THAT TIME, YOU'LL BE FORBIDDEN FROM HAVING SEX, OR EVEN MASTRBATING.
AND SHOULD YOU SUCCESSFULLY COMPLETE THIS...
...YOU MAY HAVE YOUR WAY WITH ME, ANYTIME, ANY-
GRIP.
BONK!
GRRRRR
WHO CARES?! JUST KEEP KISSING ME, MAN!
WH- ARE YOU COMPLETELY STUPID?!
I'M OFFERING YOU THE CHANCE OF A LIFETIME, AND YOU'D THROW IT AWAY FOR A FEW KISSES?!

HEY-
RELAX.
WHAT ARE YOU-
EVER SINCE I MET YOU, IT'S BEEN ONE GAME AFTER THE OTHER, HASN'T IT?
AREN'T YOU TIRED?
C'MON... BE HONEST!
ER, WELL... *COUGH*
I TAKE A LOT OF PRIDE IN MY WORK! IT'S-
WORK?!
THAT'S WHAT I MEAN!
WHEN WAS THE LAST TIME YA' SAT BACK AND RELAXED? LET SOMEONE ELSE TAKE THE WHEEL FOR A CHANGE.
BLEH.
SIGH YOU CAN BE ENDLESSLY FRUSTRATING SOME-TIMES, ELI.
MMM...
CHOMP.
...FINE.
SHREDDD!
WOAH!
PLOP!
KEEP GOING...
GRIND
MMF~
GRIND
MM!
JUST THAT LIKE~
FUCK YEAH
AH...
UNTIL EVERYTHING ELSE...
...MELTS AWAY.

HEY!
YER GETTIN' AWFUL COZY, AREN'T YA', DOC?
CLAMP!
CLAMP!
SLIDE
AND YOU SEEM TO BE "KNOCKING" AT THE DOOR OF OPPORTUNITY YET AGAIN...
BUT... IS THIS, LIKE, REALLY OKAY, DOC?
IT'S JUST-
W-WELL, YOU KNOW!
TWIST
TWIST
WOAH!
DON'T DO THAT AGAIN, IT'S SENSITIVE!
THERE!
THAT SHOULD BE ENOUGH LUBRICANT, NOW KEEP GOING.
DRIP...
HEH... EH HE-HE... HEE HAH HAH!
WHAT?!
AND JUST WHAT HAPPENED TO ALL THAT BRAVADO FROM A MINUTE AGO?
I DUNNO... I'M KINDA' BIG. I DON'T WANNA' HURT YOU BY ACCIDENT.

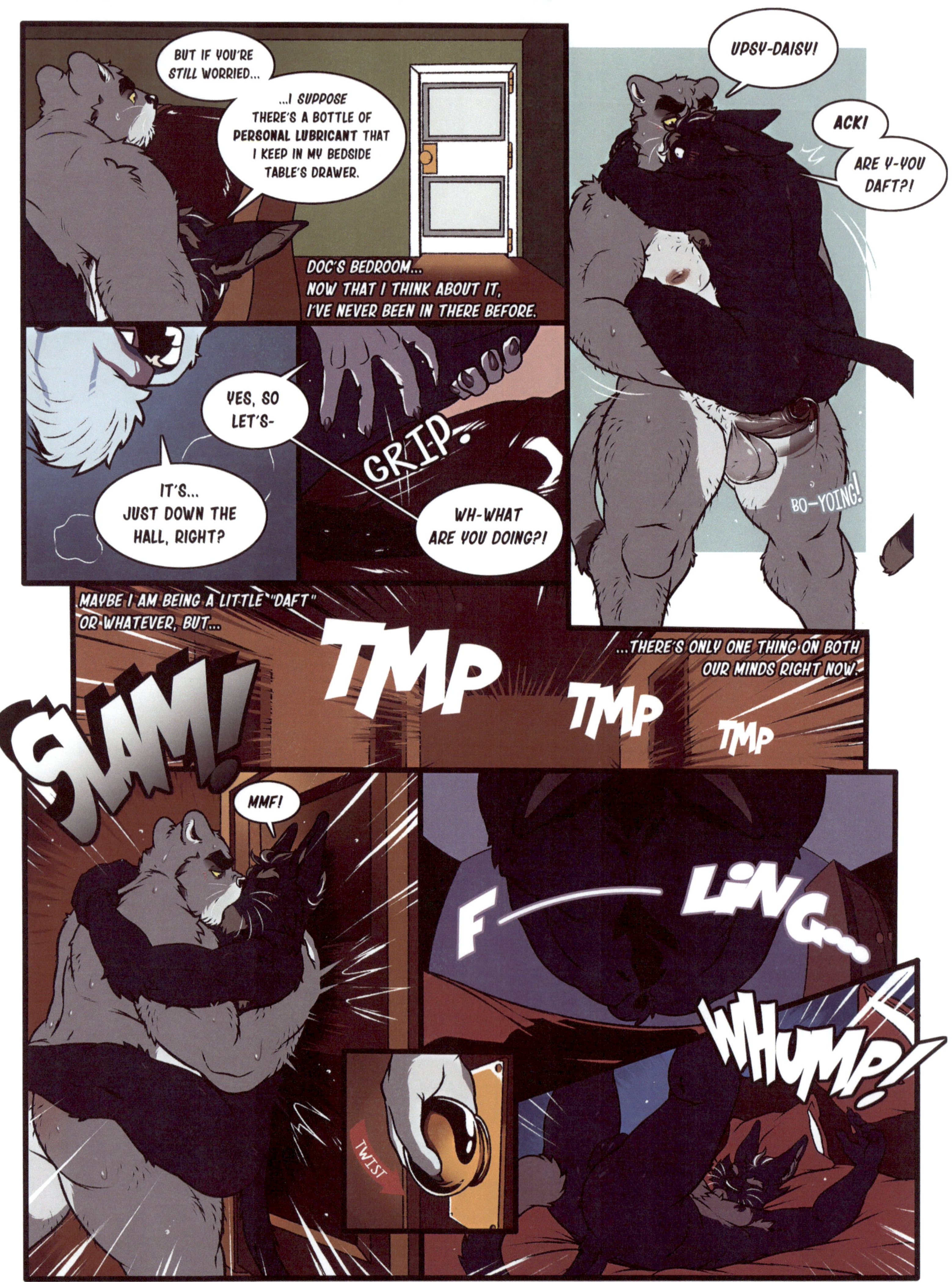

BUT IF YOU'RE STILL WORRIED...
...I SUPPOSE THERE'S A BOTTLE OF PERSONAL LUBRICANT THAT I KEEP IN MY BEDSIDE TABLE'S DRAWER.
UPSY-DAISY!
ACK!
ARE Y-YOU DAFT?!
DOC'S BEDROOM... NOW THAT I THINK ABOUT IT, I'VE NEVER BEEN IN THERE BEFORE.
YES, SO LET'S-
GRIP.
IT'S... JUST DOWN THE HALL, RIGHT?
WH-WHAT ARE YOU DOING?!
BO-YOING!
MAYBE I AM BEING A LITTLE "DAFT" OR WHATEVER, BUT...
TMP
TMP
TMP
...THERE'S ONLY ONE THING ON BOTH OUR MINDS RIGHT NOW.
SLAM!
MMF!
F-LING...
WHUMP!
TWIST

CH...
CHRIST, ELI! LET ME AT LEAST GET THE LUBE!
COME ON... COME ON! I KNOW IT'S SOMEWHERE IN THIS GOD-FORSAKEN DRAWER...
A-HA!
GRIP
ELI?!
SHFFL
SHFFL
YOINK!
FINALLY... I CAN GET A GOOD LOOK AT IT! HMM... LESS PINK THAN VERNON'S.
HAVE YOU GONE ABSOLUTELY MAD, CAT?!
SPREAD.
RELAX! FUCK... THERE'S SOMETHIN' I WANTED TO TRY BEFORE YA' USE THAT STUFF.
HOOOO...
SNIIIIFF...
HIS SMELL IS... INTOXICATING...
WHAT ARE YOU-
HNGGFF!
SLUP!
HERE GOES NOTHING...
AND THE TASTE... IT'S... IT'S...

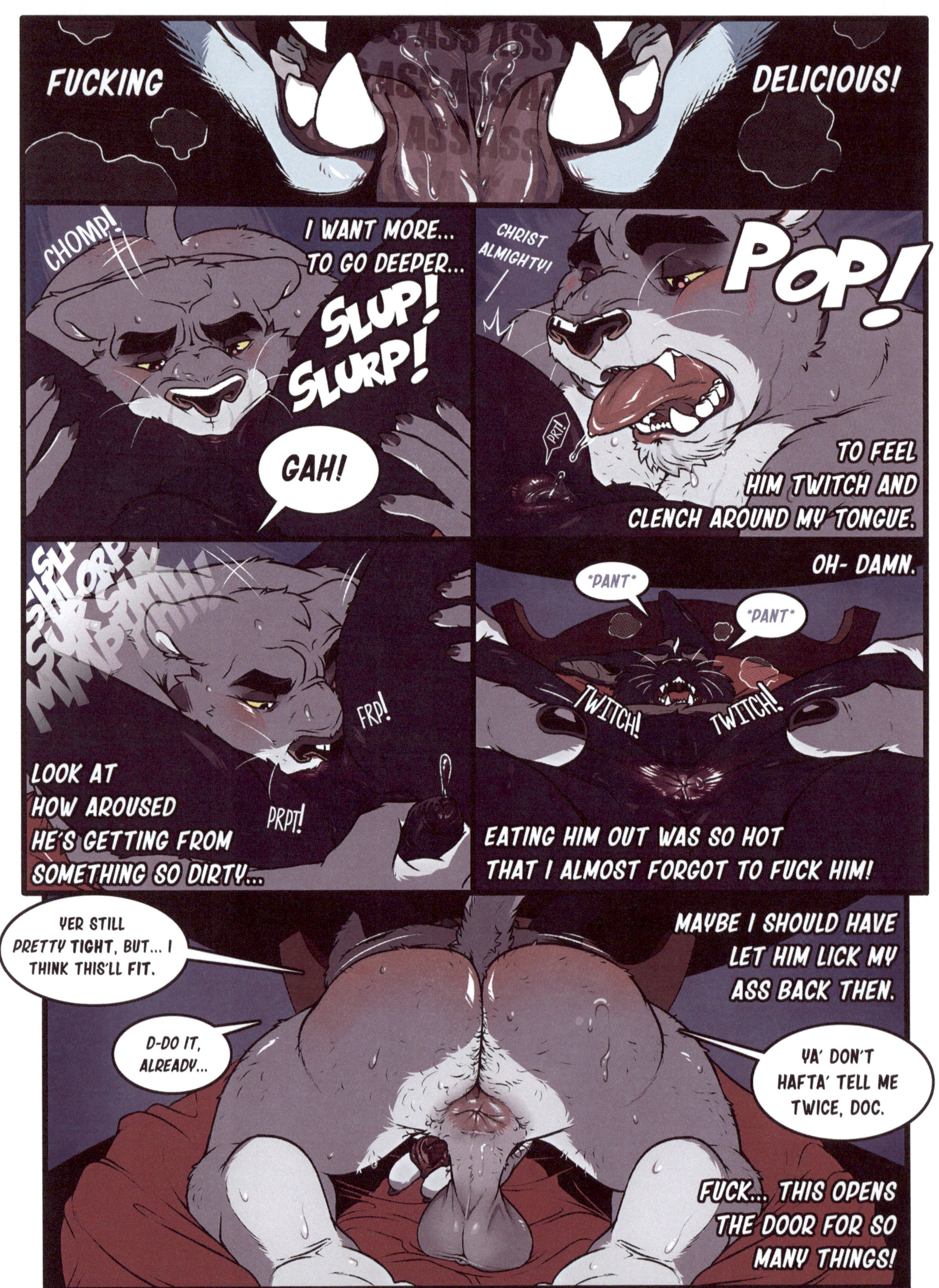

FUCKING
DELICIOUS!
CHOMP!
I WANT MORE... TO GO DEEPER...
SLUP! SLURP!
GAH!
CHRIST ALMIGHTY!
POP!
PRT!
TO FEEL HIM TWITCH AND CLENCH AROUND MY TONGUE.
SLP SLORP SLK SMK MMPHMM
FRP!
PRPT!
LOOK AT HOW AROUSED HE'S GETTING FROM SOMETHING SO DIRTY...
OH- DAMN.
PANT
PANT
TWITCH!
TWITCH!
EATING HIM OUT WAS SO HOT THAT I ALMOST FORGOT TO FUCK HIM!
YER STILL PRETTY TIGHT, BUT... I THINK THIS'LL FIT.
D-DO IT, ALREADY...
MAYBE I SHOULD HAVE LET HIM LICK MY ASS BACK THEN.
YA' DON'T HAFTA' TELL ME TWICE, DOC.
FUCK... THIS OPENS THE DOOR FOR SO MANY THINGS!

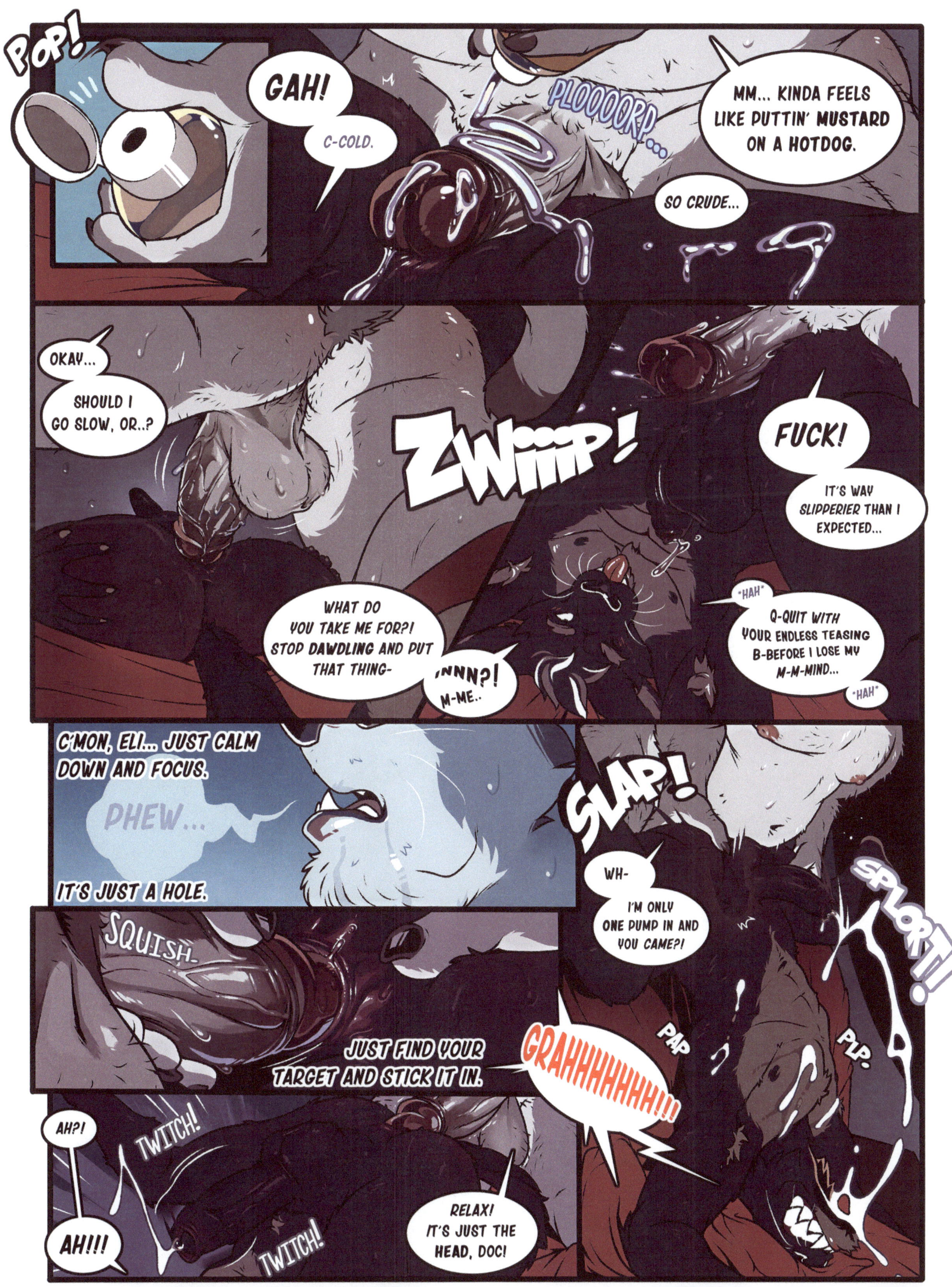

POP!
GAH!
C-COLD.
PLOOOORP...
MM... KINDA FEELS LIKE PUTTIN' MUSTARD ON A HOTDOG.
SO CRUDE...
OKAY...
SHOULD I GO SLOW, OR..?
ZWMP!
FUCK!
IT'S WAY SLIPPERIER THAN I EXPECTED...
WHAT DO YOU TAKE ME FOR?! STOP DAWDLING AND PUT THAT THING-
NNN?! M-ME..
HAH
Q-QUIT WITH YOUR ENDLESS TEASING B-BEFORE I LOSE MY M-M-MIND...
HAH
C'MON, ELI... JUST CALM DOWN AND FOCUS.
PHEW...
IT'S JUST A HOLE.
SLAP!
WH-
I'M ONLY ONE PUMP IN AND YOU CAME?!
SPLORT!!
SQUISH.
JUST FIND YOUR TARGET AND STICK IT IN.
GRAHHHHHHH!!!
PAP
PLP.
AH?!
TWITCH!
TWITCH!
RELAX! IT'S JUST THE HEAD, DOC!
AH!!!

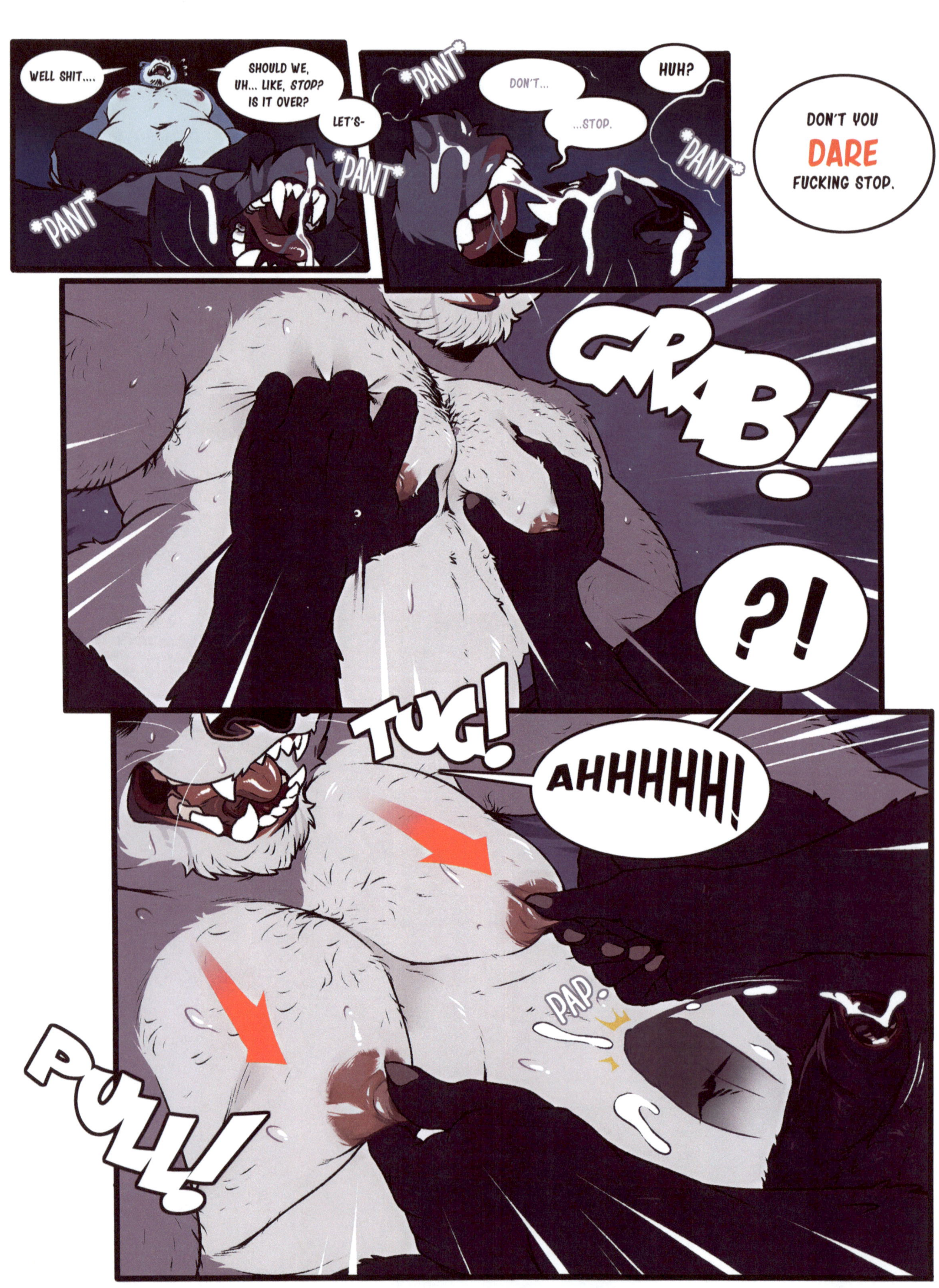

WELL SHIT....
PANT
SHOULD WE, UH... LIKE, STOP? IS IT OVER?
LET'S-
PANT
PANT
DON'T...
...STOP.
HUH?
PANT
DON'T YOU DARE FUCKING STOP.
GRAB!
?!
TUG!
AHHHHH!
PULL!
PAP.

HUFF
HUFF
GRINNNND...
YOU STARTED A JOB...
...NOW FINISH IT.
AH!
PLAP!
PLAP!
PAP PAP PAP PAP PAP
TUG!
TUG!
FLIP
PLOOP.
'KAY.
LET'S TRY IT IN THIS POSITION FOR A WHILE.

AND SO, HE RAVAGED ME.
YANK!
SLAP!
PAP PAP PAP
NICE 'N DEEP...
PUTTING ALL HIS WEIGHT ON TOP OF ME...
AH- MMF!
SQUIRT!
PLAP.
PLP.
SLAP! SLAP! SLAP!
HUFF
*GAHHHHH...!
HUFF
SPLAT!
PLP.
MAKING ME CUM AGAIN AND AGAIN, NEVER STOPPING TO REST...
*HARDER!

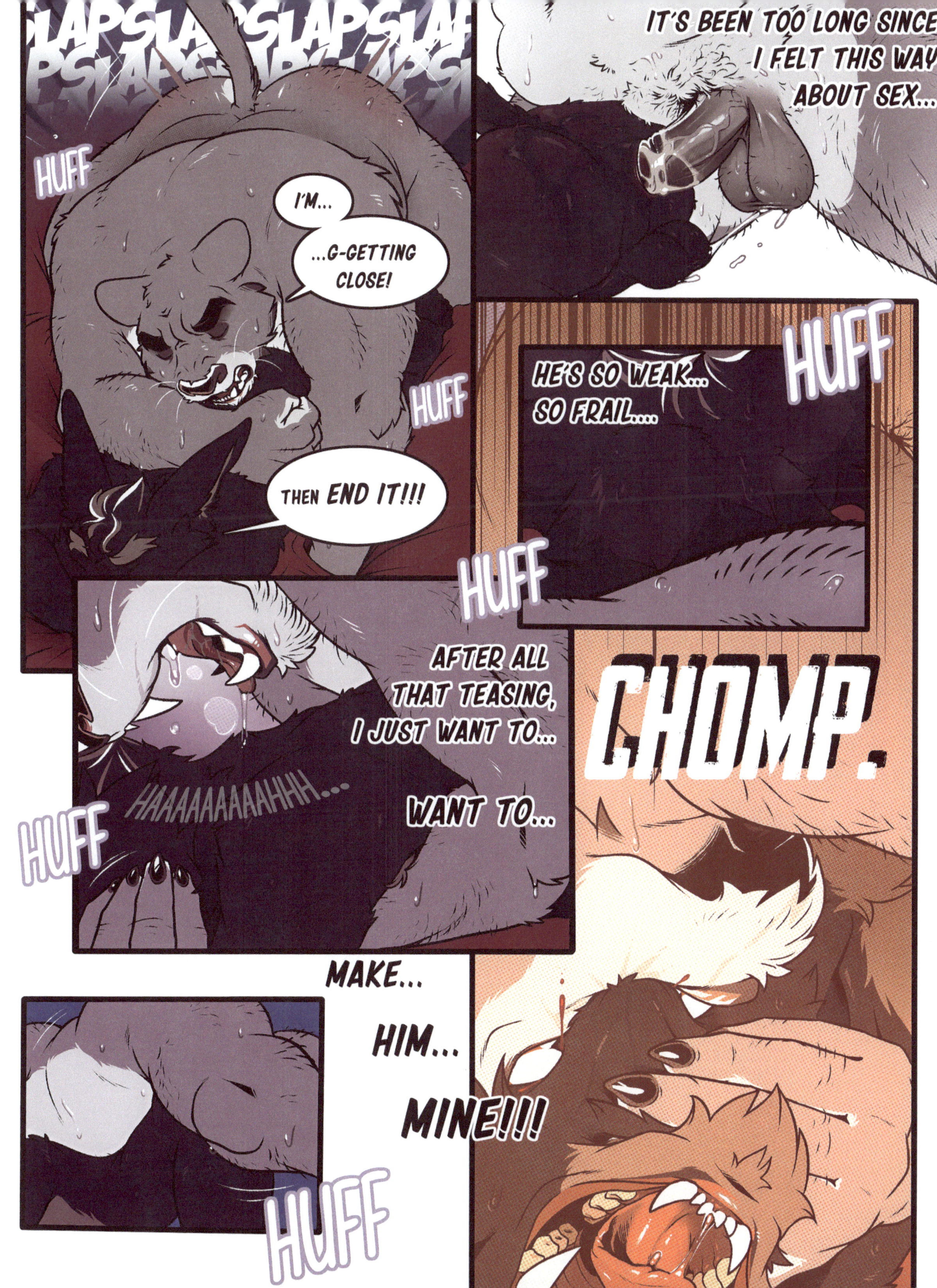

SLAP SLAP SLAP SLAP SLAP PS SLAP SLAP SLAPS
IT'S BEEN TOO LONG SINCE I FELT THIS WAY ABOUT SEX...
HUFF
I'M...
...G-GETTING CLOSE!
HUFF
THEN END IT!!!
HE'S SO WEAK... SO FRAIL....
HUFF
HUFF
AFTER ALL THAT TEASING, I JUST WANT TO...
WANT TO...
HAAAAAAAAAHHH...
HUFF
CHOMP.
MAKE...
HIM...
MINE!!!
HUFF

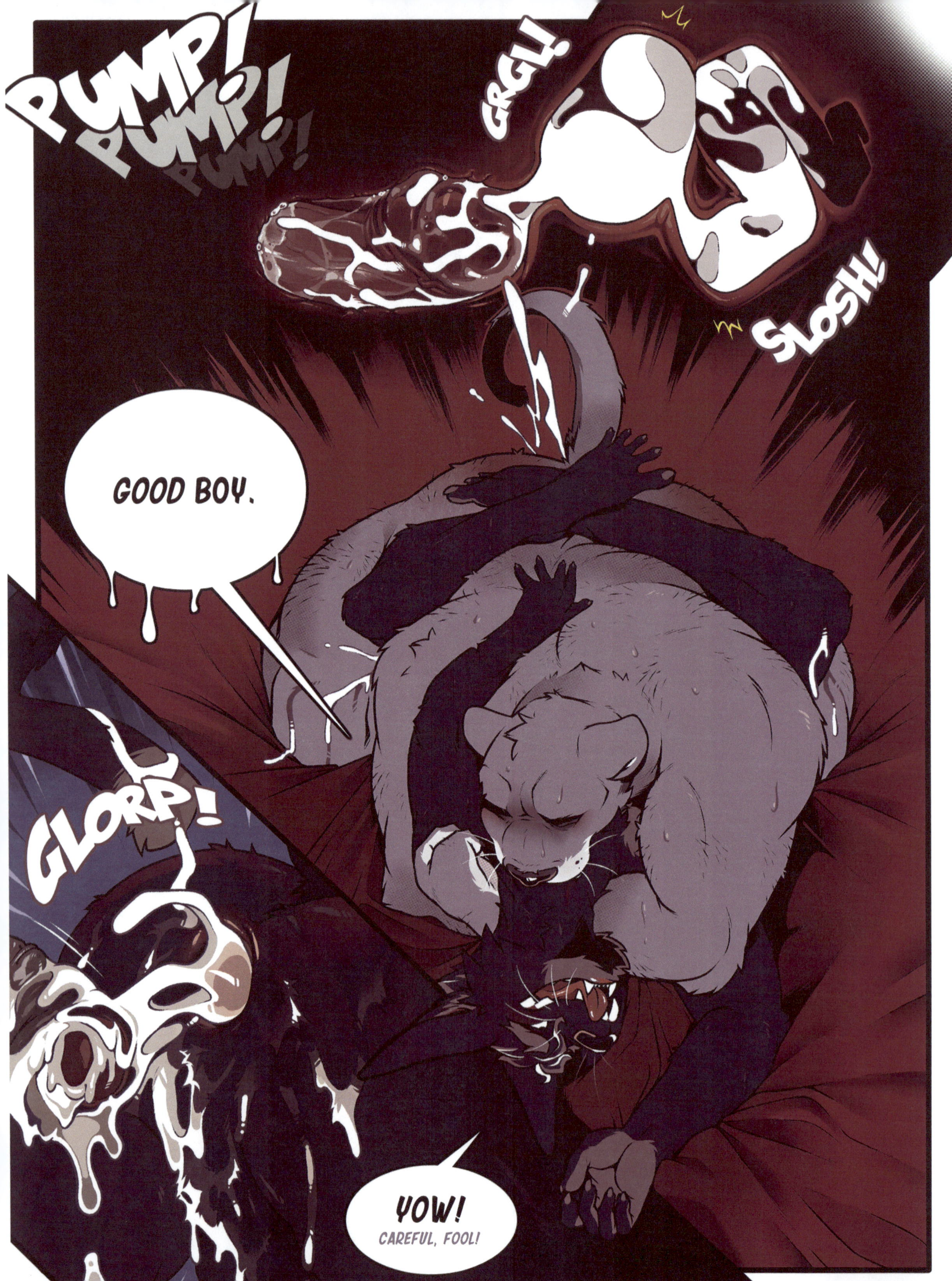

PUMP!
PUMP!
PUMP!
GRGL!
SLOSH!
GOOD BOY.
GLORP!
YOW!
CAREFUL, FOOL!

!
THAT SMARTS, DAMMIT!
DO YOU EVEN REALIZE HOW DANGEROU
SNORT
ZZZ...
ZZZZZZZ...
DROOP.
GETTING RATHER COMFY, AREN'T WE? LET'S AT LEAST SHOWER BEFORE BEDTIME.
SIGH
FWIP!
FWIP!
POP!
POP!

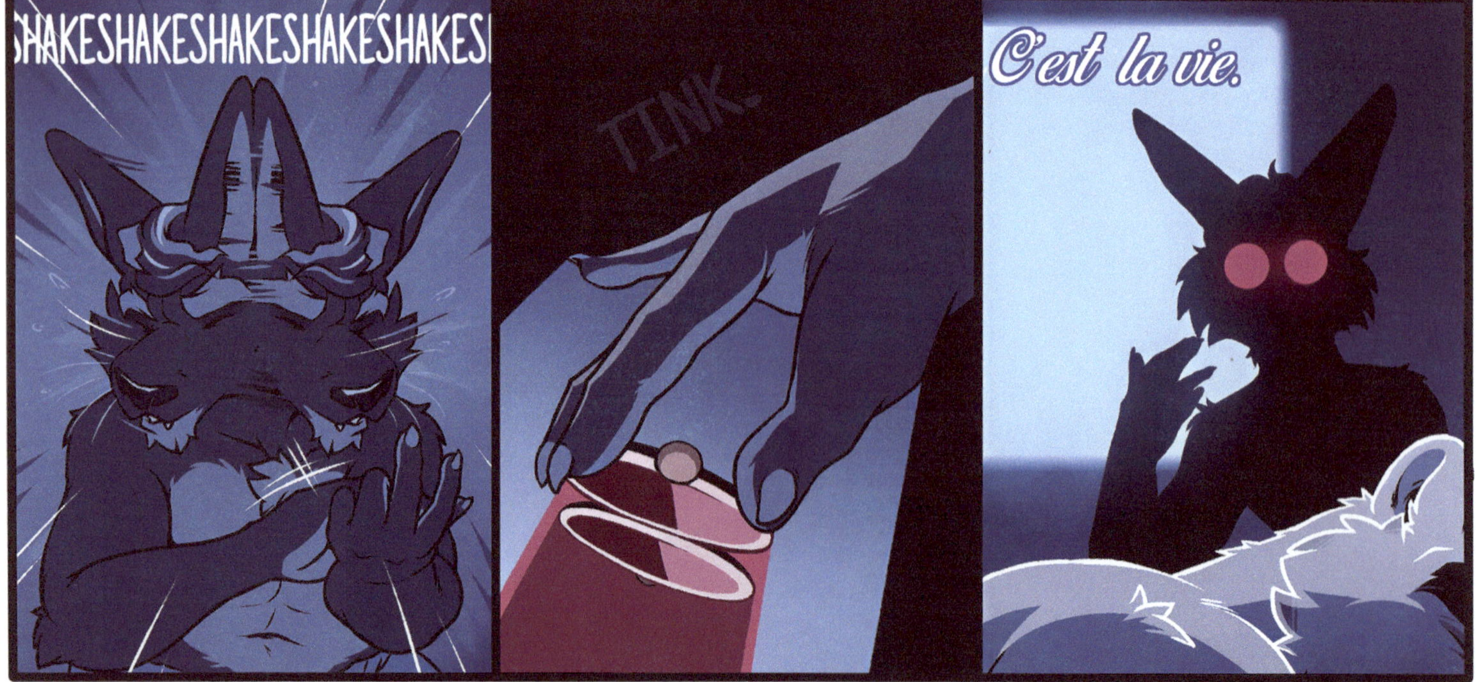

Sigh...
...THINGS HAVE ESCALATED. FASTER THAN I EVER EXPECTED.
...
IT SEEMS LIKE...
SHFF.
Why am I now imagining us...
...Having a long, loving future together?
BLINK
BLINK
SHAKESHAKESHAKESHAKESHAKES
TINK.
C'est la vie.

CHIRP...
CHIRP
CHIRP
CHIRP...
'EY, GOOD-
YAWWWWN...
FWUMP!
-MORNING..?
HMPH. I GUESS I SHOULDN'T HAVE EXPECTED HIM TO THE TOUCHY-FEELY TYPE.
STILL, HE COULD HAVE AT LEAST WAITED FOR ME TO WAKE UP.
WHY'S MY LAP FEEL SO C-
...COLD.
GLEAM!
WHAT. THE. HELL?!
DOC?!?
JINGLE~!
JINGLE~!
END OF PART ONE.

HUMP!
HUFF
HUFF
FUUUUUCK...
I WANNA FUCK SOMETHING SOOOO BAD, DOC!
BEEN CAGED AND TEASED BY DOC FOR WEEKS ON END.
HUMP!
JINGLE~
CONFUSED BUT WILLING TO PLAY ALONG WITH DOC'S ANTICS.
UM... IF I MAY OFFER AN ALTERNATIVE, MR. ELI?
PAP!
PAP!
HOLY HELL! YOU'RE GRIPPING ME LIKE CRAZY, SIR!
GRRRR...!
PAP!
K-KEEP HITTING THAT SPOT, KID! I'M GETTING CLOSE...
Captain Nikko 2024

www.ingramcontent.com/pod-product-compliance
Lightning Source LLC
Chambersburg PA
CBHW040829050726
47507CB00021B/156